WAGON TRAIN
911

Jamie Gilson

TRAIN 911

SCHOLASTIC INC.
New York Toronto London Auckland Sydney

ISBN 0-590-12053-0

Copyright © 1996 by Jamie Gilson.
All rights reserved. Published by Scholastic Inc., 555 Broadway, New York, NY 10012, by arrangement with Lothrop, Lee & Shepard Books, a division of William Morrow & Company, Inc. SCHOLASTIC and associated logos are trademarks and/or registered trademarks of Scholastic Inc.

12 11 10 9 8 7 6 5 4 3 2   9/9 0 1 2/0

Printed in the U.S.A.   40

First Scholastic printing, October 1997

To Anne and Martin
Onward!

To Anne and Martin
Onward!

# CONTENTS

D-Rex

"I won't do it," Dinah said. "I just turned eleven years old. That's too young to get married. They can't make me."

"They can, too," Kaat told her. "They do what they want to. They don't care. One of the guys in that line is your new husband. And one of them is mine. Which one do you want?"

It wasn't much of a line. Eight or nine boys were all that was left. They were standing under the basketball net at the far end of the multipurpose room. Very soon, Mr. Marconi, the fifth-grade teacher in charge, would finish calling out their names one by one.

"I'll wait till I grow up, thank you very much," Dinah said.

"How much more *up* can she grow?" Clyde, the boy in front of her, whispered out loud.

"I'll grow six feet," Dinah shot back, "and wear a different sneaker on each one."

"Ignore him," Kaat said. "He just wishes *he* could see over everybody's heads."

Dinah was five-ten, but she might just as well have been six feet tall. Not a single fifth grader came close.

"Okay, people," Mr. Marconi boomed over the mike, "only a few names left here. Hold it down."

Nobody was holding it down. Outside, little BBs of sleet had been icing the streets all day, but inside, it was hot. Kids had pulled off their sweaters and rolled them into gym floor pillows.

"Getting married's no big deal," Kaat told Dinah. "Everybody in here'll be married by noon. We'll have fun. You'll see."

Almost seventy kids—the whole fifth grade—were scattered around the big multipurpose room. Most days, kids would be at gym there. But this wasn't gym. Nobody was shooting hoops or running laps. Instead, all over the shiny floor, boys were sitting with girls. On purpose.

"I bet I get Charles. I've got my fingers crossed for Charles," Kaat said. "It's *got* to be Charles. Who do you want, really?"

"I told you, I don't believe in arranged marriages. Besides, my mother always says not to do stuff just because everybody else does."

Kaat laughed. "I'd bet that doesn't mean flunking fifth grade just because every other kid is passing it."

This was prime-time fifth grade. This was Mr. Marconi's pet project of the whole year. It was his cheer-up-the-winter-glooms project. They'd be pioneering from Missouri to Oregon for two whole weeks of January. Mr. Marconi called it Wagons Out West. For short he called it WOW.

He stood at the free-throw line shaking

his brown ten-gallon hat, mixing up the names left inside. In minutes—seconds, maybe—boys were going to reach into that hat, pull out their names, and end up married to Dinah Barnes and Kaat Jackson for two whole weeks.

"Maybe they lost our names," Kaat said. "I tell you what. If they lost them, we'll skip school, go to my house, and finish that toothpick Statue of Liberty we started last summer. It'll make 'Entertainment Tonight' and we'll get rich and famous. Okay?"

"You're on," Dinah told her. "But if they lost my name, then wishes come true. And if wishes came true, I'd be five-foot-two and this gym floor would be a cushion." She stuck her long legs between Jessica and Clyde, in front of her.

"Peeee-yew." Clyde bashed the toes of her black high-tops with his notebook. Jessica turned around and held her nose.

Dinah put both thumbs into her ears and wiggled her fingers at them. Then she pulled one foot back and rubbed her leg. "This is a pain," she said.

Clyde laughed too loud. "Dinah's sore," he called. "Wo-wo, what do ya know, the Dinahsaur is sore. What we have here is a sore D-Rex."

"A sore D-Rex," Jessica repeated.

"Some people sound like second graders," Kaat told them.

Clyde poked at Dinah's shoe with a pencil. "Dinah Barnes is a Dinahsmellus."

It wasn't exactly unfair. Dinah had been the first to call herself D-Rex. That was in fourth grade, when suddenly her long-sleeved shirts came to just below her elbows. "De D-Rex is gonna *get* you," she'd say, with a dinosaur lope to go with it.

Even now her arms and legs were clumsy-long. And her blondish hair was so fine it matted at the nape of her neck as she slept. Kaat had tried once to braid Dinah's hair into neat cornrows like her own, but halfway through, Dinah's head had looked like a pineapple and they'd collapsed into giggles.

"Settle down, people," Mr. Marconi said. "We're almost to the end. I know this is an exciting time for you. But very soon now you'll all have your partners for WOW."

The idea for WOW was, you traveled in wagon trains of five couples. Actually, you fake traveled. During WOW weeks, it was math when you bought fake lanterns and powder horns with fake money. It was science when you caught fake cholera. It was also a trip of chance. Some kids fake died. They had shorter journals.

On the first day of WOW, the girls wrote down their names and the boys picked them out of Mr. Marconi's cowboy hat so there'd be couples. The numbers had come out even. For the first time in the eight years Mr. Marconi had been doing this, everybody was going to be married. There wouldn't be any leftover boys to be lone rangers or leftover girls to travel as cranky aunts. They were a complete set.

Michael, a kid from Ms. Stefanik's class, was next in line. Mr. Marconi held the hat high so he couldn't peek in.

"All right, Michael, tell us. Who'll be your lucky wife?"

Michael grabbed a paper from the hat and, before reading it, pressed it to his forehead. "I see.... I see ahead. I see a *head.* I see curls on the head. Oh, no, no! They're not curls. They're *snakes.* It's snake hair. It's..." He dropped the paper. He clutched his throat. "Medusa!" He fell down dead.

Kids laughed and Michael loved it. They liked him. He hit home runs, kicked goals, had red hair and an easy grin. He went to everybody's birthday party.

"Medusa, arrrrg," he moaned as he writhed on the floor. Medusa was in this Greek myth they'd read. Every day was a bad hair day for Medusa. Each strand on her head was a hissing serpent. She couldn't keep friends, either: If you looked at her you turned to stone.

Mr. Marconi nudged Michael with his toe. It wasn't exactly a kick. It wasn't hard enough to count as child abuse, but it was swift enough to break the Medusa spell. Michael got up. Slowly.

A bunch of girls sitting together giggled.

"I hope he didn't pick me," Kaat said. "Charles is next in line."

"If it's me," Dinah told her, "he picked Jurassic Girl and he'll have to die all over again."

But Michael wouldn't be all that bad, she thought. He doesn't make fun of me. He doesn't say *anything* to me. I could live with that. For two weeks, anyway.

Michael unfolded the paper, stared at it, slapped his head, and groaned.

Clyde and Jessica looked back at Dinah, grinning. "Sharpen those dino-fangs," Clyde called. "Michael's going crazy. He must have picked you."

"He must have picked you," repeated Jessica.

☞And the Winner Is...

"Looks like it," Dinah told them. She started to get up.

Then Michael grinned. "Marilou Westfall," he read out loud and clear. Marilou's friends shrieked. She stood up and headed to the microphone, tossing her long black hair for anyone who might be watching. If Marilou's name had been Dinah, her friends would have called her Dynamite.

"Group," Mr. Marconi announced, putting his hands on Michael's and Marilou's shoulders. "I want you to meet

Hiram and Hepsibah, the new Mr. and Mrs. Winchester." A couple of kids whistled. This was perfect. Marilou already had Michael's name and M + M in little hearts all over her notebook.

"Hang on to this, Hepsibah." Mr. Marconi handed Marilou a big manila envelope. "Soon we'll open them and you'll find out all you need to know about your new selves. It lists all your kids—as well as all of your goats—and oxen and horses. It'll tell you where you've lived and what you did before heading out west."

Michael crooked his elbow. Marilou put her arm through it, tossed her hair twice, and they strolled into the hall to get their wedding picture taken. Most of the new couples had marched out to the camera two feet apart, at least.

"Okay, Charles is next. He's so cute. And besides, his cat just had three kittens. If you get him, will you give him to me?" Kaat asked.

"Absolutely," Dinah told her.

Dinah and Kaat had been best friends

since the middle of fourth grade when Kaat had moved to town. They weren't much alike. Kaat was dark, Dinah light; Kaat tidy, Dinah tousled; Kaat longed to be an engineer, Dinah hadn't a clue what she wanted to be. But from the start they laughed at the same things, and that did it.

"Cross your fingers and your toes," Kaat whispered.

Charles stepped up to the cowboy hat, pulled out a name, and without making a face, growling, or throwing himself on the floor, read it out loud. "Kaat Jackson," he said.

"The toes *did* it," Dinah told her, wiggling them back into place.

Kaat jumped to her feet, ran halfway to the mike, then slowed down and shrugged like she could care less.

"Say hello to Mr. and Mrs. Randolph Gates," Mr. Marconi announced. Dinah and a few kids on the other side of the room clapped as Kaat and Charles walked out—two feet apart—to get their pictures taken.

"Okay, Zach, what I want to know," the

girl behind Dinah asked, "is why the *boys* get to choose. Why can't the girls pick the names?"

"Sar-ah," the boy next to her said, "aren't you glad I pulled you out of a hat? Aren't you lucky?"

"I feel sick," Dinah said out loud.

Sarah moved up to join her. "What's the matter?"

"I want to go home. I think I've got measles."

Zach crawled forward, too. "Really?" he asked and looked at her closely. "Want to use my red marker?"

"Think it would work?"

"Nope. They'd catch you," Sarah said. "Even if you put dots all over your face and arms, they'd check your belly, too."

"Fine. Skip measles. I think I've got a tooth that hurts really bad." She rubbed her gums.

"Sure, and then some dentist'll dig caves in it."

"That," Dinah said, "would be better than getting married."

"Being married's not so bad," Sarah told her. "Yet."

"Not so bad for you," Dinah said. "I bet nobody's ever called you a praying mantis."

Sarah giggled. "One of those bugs that looks like a stick? I never heard that one. I bet it was Marilou who said it. Or her double best-friends Brandi and Tiffani. Same thing. They think they're cute and nobody else is. Zach," she said, "did you hear what Marilou said about Dinah?"

Kaat waved at Dinah with both hands as she and Charles came back from picture taking. When they sat down, though, it was on the other side of the room with Charles's friends.

Meantime, the picking went on until there were only two boys left in line, and still no one had gotten Dinah.

All of the important girls' names were gone. No need for most kids to listen anymore. The room echoed. It sounded like reds against blues with the score tied ten-ten.

"People," Mr. Marconi whispered into the microphone, "this is a warning." His whisper boomed. "WOW depends upon your complete cooperation. If you want to cancel the whole program, just keep right on talking."

He'd never do it. This was his WOW. Still, why take a chance? The gym got quiet.

"Hey, you guys, it's Orin Philpot's turn," Zach said. "The dork's up to bat."

Dinah stared at her sneakers. They were size elevens, Dinah size.

"Not Orin Philpot," she told the shoes. She closed her eyes and dug her knuckles into her eyelids so all she could see was a black hole with sharp white stars in it flashing like sparklers.

Star light, star bright, she thought, I wish I may, I wish I might, have this wish I wish...right now. Just this once, stars. Don't make me marry Orin Philpot. If I have to marry Orin Philpot I will die.

Dinah kept her eyes clamped shut as Orin stepped up to the microphone.

Except for a few giggles, the room was quiet.

Mr. Marconi didn't have to hold the hat high for Orin. Orin looked like he was still in second grade. He was almost five feet tall—with shoes on. His mother said he was all skin and bones.

Dinah Barnes had bones, too. "Big bones," her mother told people. "Someday she'll be tall and willowy like her aunt Phyllis. But she'll always be my baby."

Mr. Marconi tilted the microphone down so Orin could read the name into it.

"Use your outdoor voice," he said.

Orin unfolded the small piece of yellow paper and looked at it. He blew in the microphone, testing it for sound, but he didn't say anything. Instead, he took the yellow paper and carefully crumpled it into a ball. He tossed the ball high in the air, tilted his head back, and opened his mouth—wide.

The whole fifth grade watched quietly. At first. Then they sucked in their breath. And finally, they began to whoop.

"What happened?" Dinah opened her eyes. She could still see the stars she'd wished on. "What's funny? Who'd he get?"

"Orin..." Sarah could hardly say it. "Orin threw... And then he..."

Kids were kicking the floor so hard it shook. "He what?" Dinah asked.

Sarah grabbed her by the arm. "He ate it," she gasped. "He *ate* it."

"Ate what?"

"He ate the yellow paper. Now he can say *he* picked Medusa and nobody'll know the difference."

Dinah closed her eyes again. Orin was the one who'd called her a praying mantis. That was after he'd missed a ball by a mile and she'd called him a wimpy shrimp.

Orin Philpot had picked her name and she knew exactly what he was thinking. He was thinking, If I am stuck with that tall insect for two weeks, I will die.

"He won't get away with it," Zach said. "You'll see."

"What if he throws it up?" Dinah asked.

"I don't think he swallowed it." Sarah frowned. "I bet it's still in his mouth, mixed in with bubble gum."

"Orin," Mr. Marconi shook the microphone at him, "That's red dish mute bus."

Or something. Dinah couldn't tell what Mr. Marconi had said. She couldn't hear him because kids were still beating their feet on the floor. WOW or not, this was too good to be quiet about.

"That's enough," Mr. Marconi announced.

"People!" Ms. Stefanik shouted from the sidelines.

Clyde and Jessica swung around to face Dinah.

"So, what do you do now, D-Rex?" Clyde asked her.

"So, what?" Jessica echoed.

Even if Orin wasn't the one, Dinah knew everyone thought he was. Why else would he have eaten the name?

"Only thing I *can* do, I guess." Dinah stretched her mouth into a huge grin, her top teeth pulled down toward her jaw. She stood up, curled her hands into Tyrannosaurus claws, and did her prehistoric lope toward the microphone.

Then she started to sing. "Here comes the bride, too tall to hide. There waits the groom, on the weh-aay to his dooooooom." But the kids were all laughing so hard that nobody heard.

3

☞That Cute Jones Family

"**M**y dear, you're all red. Do you have a fever?" Ms. Stefanik put the back of her hand on Dinah's forehead. "No, you feel cool enough. Maybe it's the excitement. Now sit up straight. Smooth your hair."

Dinah slumped in the chair and pulled her red-striped T-shirt over the knees of her jeans. Then she scraped her light, wispy hair forward with her fingers. This was her wedding picture.

The camera pointed at her, and cameras were not her friend. They always saw her wrong. In the class picture, she stood a head above the other kids in the back row. She looked like a spare teacher, maybe, on an off day, in a Mickey Mouse T-shirt.

For this one, Orin was standing next to Dinah, so his head was higher. Ms. Stefanik had told him to rest his hand on her shoulder, the way people used to in portraits. But Orin's hand didn't touch her shoulder. It hovered about an inch away— to keep cooties at bay, Dinah figured.

"Don't worry. It's not catching," she told him.

Orin licked his palm and pressed his hand hard on his sandy cowlick, but as soon as he let go, the hair popped up again.

"Well, my dears." said Ms. Stefanik, "I see that you're the Jones family now— Lydia and Martin. This is the picture you'd give your friends and relatives back East to remember you by. Don't smile. They didn't smile in those days, not for formal pictures."

"Hey, D-Rex," a kid at the drinking fountain called, "you catch yourself an itty-bitty dino-bite shrimp?"

Dinah didn't smile. But just as the shutter clicked, she gave the kid her best D-Rex look. Lapping her bottom teeth over her top lip, she opened her eyes wide as though she were about to crunch a tasty morsel named Orin.

"Rrrrrrrrrr," she growled quietly. She was a carnivore Dinahsaurus. Or a hungry bug. Praying mantises eat each other up for snacks. Orin said so.

Orin hadn't seen the D-Rex starving-mantis face. Neither, it appeared, had Ms. Stefanik.

"Perfect," she said. "Who's next?" Two more kids stepped up. "Congratulations. Smooth your hair. Don't smile."

They posed without smiling, but when the camera snapped they both giggled.

"Did you make a face?" Dinah asked Orin as they headed back to the gym.

"I didn't need to," he told her. "I've already got one."

Very funny. Dinah closed her eyes. The stars were gone. They were traitors, anyway. Look what they'd done, even after she'd told them she'd die if she had to marry him.

"Hey," Dinah said, "if you shut your eyes, you can still see the flash from the camera. It's like a floating orange box."

Orin stopped walking and closed his eyes. "Mine isn't an orange box. It's a yellow sign. It says 'Slow Children.'"

He meant her. She knew it. She was taller, but he thought he was big-time smarter, and he didn't keep it to himself. He was going to be a gnat in her nose for two whole weeks.

"You eat yellow paper a lot?" she asked him. "It might go down easier with peanut butter."

"I mostly save it for holidays," he told her. "But with your name on it, I thought this particular piece might have supernatural qualities."

Orin talked like that. Kids rolled their eyes and groaned at his oral reports. They were filled with stuff like "this particular piece" and "supernatural qualities."

"Supernatural qualities? Like it might

make you disappear? Or I might get the two-week black plague?"

"Actually," Orin told her, "I thought with your autograph on that particular piece, it might make me tall. Besides, paper is fiber. Fiber makes you grow. It's a scientific fact." He sighed. "On television it would have worked."

Back in the gym, kids were spread out on the floor. Mr. Marconi was trying to get their attention.

"Sarah told me you cheated," Dinah told Orin. "She said you just chewed my name into your Dubble Bubble."

"Not true. I ground it into minute bits and swallowed it."

"All right, folks, listen up," Mr. Marconi said. "I want you to open those envelopes, take out the tags with your new names on them, and hang them around your necks. All the time you wear them, that's what people will call you. And you'll wear them most of the time at school for the next two weeks."

"Yuck! Triple yuck! Can I change my

name?" a girl called. "Nobody's name is Charity."

"May I be excused from the whole enterprise?" Orin asked. "No, I guess not."

"Next," Mr. Marconi went on, "read the paper that tells all about you as a couple. Talk about it. Think about it. Only come up here to ask genuinely important questions. No, Brandi, you may not change your name."

Dinah took out her tag, hung it around her neck, and looked down. It said ꓢƎNOႦ ⱯIᗡ⅄⅃. She handed the folder to Orin.

"Okay, on TV, that paper you ate would have made you into a tall soap star with a square chin, and you know what else? On the way to the mike I would have shrunk into a tiny cheerleader with bouncy black hair."

"We would have been transformed."

"We would have been cartoons."

"We are now," he said.

That wasn't nice. It wasn't fair. Dinah looked down at her size elevens.

Nobody else was looking; they were all

reading about who they were going to be for two weeks. There were squeals and groans all over the multipurpose room.

Dinah and Orin sat down in a corner. Orin opened the envelope, pulled out the paper, and read, "Martin and Lydia Jones from Philadelphia. We're married one year. No kids. I'm twenty-six years old. A doctor. My first wife died when our house burned down. Then I married you."

Dinah looked over his shoulder. "I'm only twenty. Oh, no. This isn't fair. I'm going to have a baby. Due in July. That's a long time, isn't it? We'll be in Oregon by then, won't we?"

"Look at this. We've got four oxen, a horse, and twenty-five head of cattle."

"Lydia sold ribbons and buttons in a shop. Her eight-year-old brother's coming with them. Well, forget that. Why does her brother have to come?"

"Martin's six foot two," Orin said. "His friends call him Big Marty."

"Where does it say that?" Dinah asked.

Orin shrugged. "*I* say it."

"Four little boys," somebody near them called out. "No way. They'll fight all the time."

"Okay, listen up, folks," Mr. Marconi said into the microphone. "I want no more complaining about who your husband or wife is. You'll come to love each other, I guarantee it. People grow close in hard times."

"I'm a farmer from Ohio," Michael told them. "I like that."

"I'm the youngest of nine children and I know how to milk cows. Bummer," Marilou said. "Michael, hurry, let's move over with Brandi and Tiffani."

"*Lydia's* small and fragile like a porcelain doll," Dinah told Orin. "She's adorable. Her friends call her..."

"Shrimp," Orin said.

"That's not adorable."

"I've noticed," Orin told her. "Human shrimp are not adored."

"You know what?" Dinah said. "Eating that paper worked. You're a tall Martin. I'm a short Lydia." She tore a piece of paper from her notebook, crumpled it up, and handed it to him. "You want to try for rich and famous?"

"What now?" Michael asked.

"Now," Mr. Marconi announced. "Now that you know who you are, I'll tell you *when* it is. As you no doubt remember from your reading, the big move west began in 1843. This is March 1846. There've been thousands of pioneers who've made the trip before you."

"That brother of yours," Orin whispered, "what's his name?"

"In WOW time, every day of school is a new month as soon as your actual trip begins," Mr. Marconi went on.

"Time flies when you're having a good time," Dinah told Orin. "We call him Buster," she went on. "He can wiggle his ears, curl his tongue, and speak three languages. He is *very* well behaved. You'll love him."

Orin counted on his fingers. "Lydia, you'd better start breathing lessons. You're going to have a baby on the road."

"Listen up, people, this is important," Mr. Marconi said. "As you know, except for fifteen minutes in the morning, you won't be in your regular rooms. You'll be with your wagon trains. So I want you to talk to other families, find out what other people do for a living and who you'd feel comfortable traveling with. Then form yourselves into wagon trains of ten people—five couples each. Go for it."

Kids all around the gym went for it, waving and yelling, locking in their friends fast.

"This is going to be a blast," said Michael.

"This is really, really awful," Marilou told him. "All the good girls are sitting on the other side of the gym. I bet they're all taken."

"Does that mean," Orin asked Dinah, "that you are not a good girl?"

"Do you see Kaat and Charles anywhere?" she asked him.

He peered across the room. "There. With that group by the free-throw line.

They look," he said, "as if they're signing their names on something."

Dinah shrugged. "Oh, well. Anybody you want to go with?"

He shook his head.

"I have a feeling," she said, "that this cute Jones family from Philadelphia is heading West tomorrow all by itself."

4

☞You Mean You with Us?

"**I**f we don't make a wagon train," Orin told Dinah, "here's what we do. We split up. You go to Chicago and see if the 1846 Bulls want a good tall forward. I'll stay in Missouri, invent virtual reality, and we'll change the course of history. Agreed?"

Kids were running and yelling, but nobody was running to them, yelling, "We need *you*."

"Good thinking," she said. "We do that and there'd be a lot less chance we'd get cholera. But, A, if I can't slam dunk in jeans, I couldn't do it in petticoats; and B, if you talked virtual reality in 1846, they'd lock you up with all the other short weird people. Besides, Lydia is tiny and cute and Martin is tall and possibly handsome. We're both terrific. Everybody should want us."

"No one seems to have noticed," Orin said. "They still think you walk on stilts and make extremely dumb faces. They look at me and think I'm..."

"A dork," Dinah said.

"A dork." Orin sighed. "School was meant for normal people. I predict nobody's going to ask us just for us. Do we have anything the normal people need? What's on our list again?"

Dinah dug it out of the envelope.

"Oxen," she said. "Say, Orin, think about it..."

"Martin," he told her. "Not Orin. They call me Big Marty, remember?"

"Okay. Martin. Besides being cute, I think you and I are rich. You must have struck gold as a doctor. I know I didn't do it selling buttons. We've got four oxen, a horse, and twenty-five head of cattle. Isn't that good?"

"That's excellent. Better than a Cadillac. Let's try it. Oh, Michael!"

"And don't talk like a teacher, Orin. You'll scare him away."

"Well, don't you make faces. Nobody wants prehistoric rabies."

Michael was just standing there staring at his sheet of paper.

"How you doing?" Orin asked him.

Dinah put on a grin and held it in place as if it were stapled there.

"I'm not sure," Michael told them. "We've got Clyde and Jessica. They said they didn't care whose team they were on, but they'd be on ours. They both worked in a textile mill in Massachusetts. They've got an eight-year-old kid. They said the kid worked there, too, but that must be a mistake. We've maybe got Sarah and Zach, but they're shopping around. Marilou's on the other side of the gym. She's trying to get Brandi and Tiffani to drop out of their wagon train and come with us."

"Do you have any oxen?" Orin asked him. "Oxen are almost essential for a..."

Dinah poked him. He started again. "You need oxen to pull the wagons. Horses don't have the stamina."

Dinah rolled her eyes, but she held her smile.

"We've got cows, a pair of mules, and a bunch of goats and chickens," Michael said. "Hey, you guys," he called, "you got any oxen or horses?"

"One horse, two pack mules," Jessica read from the list, "and some pigs. Clyde says this is so dumb. I think so, too."

"Erase the grin," Orin whispered to Dinah. "You look like you plan to rob them the first night out. Try normal."

Dinah relaxed her face and dropped her shoulders. Who did Orin think he was, anyway, telling her what to do?

Sarah and Zach hurried over from the far side of the big room. "Those kids are trying to get twelve and fourteen people in their wagon trains, but Mr. Marconi says no way," Sarah told them. "Even though you've got Marilou, we'll stick with you, Michael."

"Good move," Michael said. "Besides, she's nice."

Sarah rolled her eyes. "Cute. All she is is cute."

"Excuse me. What are your occupations?" Orin asked them. "I mean, what do you do?"

"I *know* what an occupation is. I'm a blacksmith. Zach the blacksmith."

"I've got five kids," Sarah said. "Five. I think that's what I do. I think I'll wait till Oregon to get an outside job."

"Any horses or oxen?" Dinah asked.

Sarah and Zach checked their list. "We've got two horses, three cows, and two pigs. That's great, isn't it? I mean, isn't cows where cottage cheese comes from? And bacon is from pigs. BLTs by the campfire."

"Oxen are best for pulling covered wagons," Dinah said. "*We* are the Joneses. And we've got four of them."

"You've also got a shrimp," said Zach. "That'll slow you down." He patted Orin on the head and laughed. "Who you going with?"

"And Martin is a doctor," Dinah went on.
"Martin?"

"Check out his name tag," Dinah said.
"Dr. Martin Jones. Anybody here pregnant?"

"Anybody what?" Marilou asked as she joined the group. "What are you *talking* about?" She didn't look at Dinah. "Michael, what have you been doing? I've been over there trying to get us in the really, really good wagon trains, but Mr. Marconi has these stupid rules. He won't let us make them any bigger than ten. It's not fair. Did you find anybody decent?"

"All right, people," Mr. Marconi announced. "Calm down, now." He waved a paper over his head. "I've got here a list of the ten people signed up for Wagon Train One." A group of kids clapped and yelled.

"And here's another complete traveling party." More cheers. "You're Train Number Two. Congratulations. I hope you're all choosing your companions well. You've got two thousand plus miles to travel together. A week from Friday we'll find out who made it West and who didn't."

"What's that supposed to mean?" Orin asked. "He's going to kill us off?"

"Sure," said Sarah. "My brother did this two years ago. He said it was a blast. But somewhere at the end you've got to throw dice to see if you live through an avalanche or not. Justin lived."

A boy rushed up with names of the kids in Wagon Train Three. "This is progress," Mr. Marconi went on, "but I need more. The rest of you, speed it up, so you can start buying supplies."

"What happens to the ones who die?" Orin asked Sarah.

"Got me," she said.

"I count eight of us. How about it?" Dinah asked.

Marilou turned to her. "How about what? You mean *you* with *us*?"

"This may be a big mistake," Sarah told Zach. "Marilou whines all the time."

"Thanks a lot," Marilou said. "Well, I refuse to be with Dinah. She's always making stupid faces."

"This is you," Dinah told her and stuck out her bottom lip in a fat pout.

"You wish."

"I'm not having fun," Zach said. "Mr. Marconi said this was going to be fun."

"Come on, Jessica." Clyde pulled at her sleeve. "Let's go somewhere else. This train is a loser."

"A real loser," said Jessica.

"We need two more people to make ten. Anybody free?" Orin called.

Mr. Marconi waved another paper in the air. "I have here Wagon Train Four complete." More kids lined up in front of him. "And Wagon Trains Five and Six. This is wonderful. Unless my math skills fail me, there are only eight more students in fifth grade. Have you found one another? Where are you? I'm waiting."

Orin began writing down their names.

"Oh, great," Marilou moaned, "I'm stuck with the leftovers."

"The Red Hot Remainders," Orin said. "Marilou, what's your last name?"

"Once again, I'm waiting," Mr. Marconi

boomed out over the mike. "And keep it down. I hope all this is friendly conversation that I'm hearing. Remember, the biggest problem the pioneers had was getting along with each other."

"I was right," Sarah said, "this is a big mistake."

"People, I'm waiting," Mr. Marconi announced. "I'm waiting."

Dinah raised her hand. "Waiter," she called. "Over here. Party of eight."

Bilkum and Moore General Store

"You folks in need? I'm a friend, indeed. You do as I say and this trip of yours will be a summer breeze."

Mr. Marconi was wearing his ten-gallon hat and a fake thin moustache. The nametag that hung from his neck said B. Bilkum. "Barney Bilkum's my name," he went on, twisting the tip of his moustache. "Supplies are my game. I'm your very best friend here at the gateway to the Great West. Ask me anything. There's nothing I don't know. Welcome one and all to Bilkum and Moore General

Store. Step right in, ladies and gents."

The General Store was in Mr. Marconi's classroom. All afternoon, while the rest of the fifth grade wrote in journals and studied maps, kids had filed into his room to buy supplies for their trip. Wagon Train Seven had been waiting in the hall for five minutes for train number six to finish. It was finally time.

They stepped right in.

"I wish we didn't have to do this," Marilou said. "I was just getting into my journal. I was telling it my innermost thoughts and feelings about going West. I was telling it this is the biggest bummer of all time."

"Mr. Marconi." Orin raised his hand. "Are we supposed to spend all our money?"

"Name's Bilkum," Mr. Marconi told him. "Don't know that other fellow you're talkin' about." He looked down at Orin's tag. "Dr. Jones, is it? Well, doctor, you talk about money, I sure as shootin' can help you out there. I hear you folks got eight hundred dollars a couple. My advice to you is to spend every last penny of it with me."

He handed each couple a sheet of paper with a long list of items on it. "This is my excellent inventory. It tells what I've got that you want and how much it'll cost you."

"I don't trust him," Dinah whispered to Orin.

"He's our teacher," Orin said.

"He is not. He's Barney Bilkum."

"You seem like intelligent folks. When you cast your eyes down that list I know you're going to pick up on my big blue bottles of Moore's Super Elixir."

"What's it for?" Sarah asked him.

"For? What's it *not* for? You get sick along the way and you take a swig of my super-duper elixir. It'll cure your chilblains, your cholera, your pains of childbirth, your toothache, your cracked collarbone. It'll dee-stroy your dysentery. It'll perk you up after a long hot day on the trail. Only five dollars. A bargain at half the price. Mark number thirteen on your list with the number of bottles you require. I recommend you get at least twenty."

"Is there any other place in town we can shop?" Dinah asked him.

"None, little lady," Barney Bilkum told her. "I'm the only show in town, and if you're sassy with me, I won't sell to you, and then, Mrs. Lydia Jones, you'd be in a pretty pickle."

"The store is called Bilkum and Moore," Dinah went on. "Where is Mr. Moore?"

"He skipped. That is to say, he moved on. Next question?"

Michael raised his hand. "My wife Hepsibah here doesn't want to go on this trip. And I think it's pretty risky, too. What should we buy to make sure we get there?"

"Use your head, Hiram Winchester, use your head. Speaking of which, I'm going to let you in on a real deal: gen-u-ine goose-feather pillows to rest your head on underneath the stars. Five bucks each, two for twelve dollars."

"That's no deal," Orin said.

"And seeds!" Barney Bilkum kept going. "I've got seeds that'll grow you tomatoes the size of my head. Only one dollar per package."

Jessica and Clyde were talking together. "Is there a guarantee?" Clyde asked.

Barney Bilkum chuckled. "No guarantee. No money back. You'll be way out there. I'll be way back here. I'm never going to see you again. You've got my word on that."

"Hey, Sarah...," Zach started.

"Use your pioneer names," Mr. Marconi said. "Don't answer unless someone calls you by your pioneer name. And keep those supply lists. You won't get real fifty-pound sacks of flour. That list is what you'll take with you. Carry on, Johann."

"Hey, Clara," Zach went on. "I've filled out the list. What do you think? I more or less took one of every other thing. I didn't get a cradle, a churn, or beans. We don't have any babies, somebody else can make the butter, and I don't like beans. Okay with you?"

"You've spent bags more than eight hundred dollars, *Johann,*" Sarah said. "Besides, *I* like beans. I say we get them."

"Mr. Marconi," Zach called.

"Who?"

"Okay. Mr. Bilkum. It's eight hundred dollars each *person.* Am I right or am I right?"

"You are wrong, sir."

"And, Johann," Sarah told him, "you bought four bottles of that stupid elixir. That's twenty dollars."

"We're going to be on the road a long time. He said it cured everything."

"That was like a commercial. It didn't *mean* anything." She drew a line through Moore's Super Elixir.

"You crossed them all out! You crossed out my medicine. If I die it's your fault."

"Make up your minds, folks," Barney Bilkum warned them. "Only twelve and a half more minutes and the Bilkum and Moore general store closes for good. Make your picks and don't spend more than your eight hundred dollars. I don't give credit."

"He's got a cradle for ten dollars," Orin said.

"We can buy a lot of flour and dried apples for that," Dinah told him. "I'll just hold the baby. She can't weigh much."

"She?"

"Right. I decided. Mildred, after my mother."

"Erika, after mine."

They spent six hundred eighty-two dollars for beans, sugar, flour, bacon, blankets, candles, matches, a saw, a knife and a whetstone, a rifle, horns of gunpowder, and more, but not much more.

"I don't like guns. Do we have to get a rifle?" Orin asked her.

"If we're going to eat buffalo and rattlesnakes, *I'm* not going to wrestle them down. Are you?"

"I, personally, am buying at *least* one gun," said Marilou, tossing her hair. "It's a jungle out there. Or a prairie, anyway. And, besides, my husband's a really, really good shot. He's going to protect me. Right?"

Michael grinned, bowed, and then aimed an imaginary rifle at the ceiling. "Pow! Pow!" he said. "Four roast ducks in two shots for dinner."

"Is one pair of snowshoes enough?" Orin asked Dinah.

"We'll share."

"And one last thing." Orin checked number forty-three on the supplies list and held it out to her.

"A pump organ? Orin Philpot, use your head. That's on the list to trap you. Look how much it costs. And it weighs a ton. Our wagon would get swallowed whole in quicksand."

Orin smiled. "What do you need money for on the road? They hadn't built malls yet. Besides, Big Marty the doctor is also Martin the Magnificent, master of the pump organ. I bet this one is carved mahogany with ebony and ivory keys. I'll give open-air concerts. We'll charge admission."

"Okay, *one* bottle of elixir," Sarah told Zach.

"Three, and that's final," Zach said.

"Time's just about up, people," Barney Bilkum called, sounding very much like Mr. Marconi.

"Use your head, Orin the Ordinary. Who's going to pay to hear it?"

"We'll be the only ones to have one. We'll be unique."

"We're unique enough."

"Time, folks."

"I give up," Dinah said. "It's just school." She underlined it on the sheet. "One really useless mahogany pump organ. Eighty dollars down the drain."

"That's it, people," Mr. Marconi announced, totally himself again. "Hand in your lists. I'll check them over to see how you've done and give them back to you in the morning. Tomorrow is the ides of March and you're on your way. Good luck. And unless you stop all this arguing, you're going to need it."

☞ Choose One

"**W**ell, good afternoon, Wagon Train Seven. Just arrange yourselves in a circle in the middle of the room."

The desks in Ms. Stefanik's room had been pushed against the walls and windows, so there was plenty of space. Wagon Train Seven sat themselves on the floor in a sort of circle. But Wagon Train Seven did not say good afternoon back. The person who greeted them was not Ms. Stefanik.

It was two o'clock, almost the end of day two of WOW. Except for lunch, Wagon

Train Seven had been together all day, learning what covered wagons were like, getting wrong answers to pioneer story problems in math, calling each other by their new, strange names. They were tired of each other.

And this woman who was smiling at them now was new. They did not want to know her.

"Glad to see you all made it to school through the blizzard. As Mr. Marconi has told you, I'm Meg. I'm going to help you through your trip out West."

Meg was about five foot two, even in cowboy boots. A green plaid shirt hung over her jeans. Her long, dark hair was pulled back with a red bandanna. And she was smiling like she thought this was fun.

"She looks about eighteen years old," Dinah whispered to Sarah.

"So do you," Sarah told her.

Dinah puckered up her face and bent her shoulders low as if she were a hundred and one. She was starting to cackle like an old crone when Orin jabbed her in the ribs.

"As you may know," Meg went on, "I'm a senior in the drama department at the university. I'm going to be part of your Wagons Out West program and you'll be part of my creative dramatics project."

This did not sound promising.

"Like we're some kind of experiment?" Marilou asked.

"In that I've never done this before, yes," Meg said.

All the other fifth-grade kids were in other rooms, doing math or art or reading stuff about Kansas in the old days. Wagon Train Seven was the last group to meet with Meg.

"What we'll do in here for thirty minutes every afternoon is move you forward on your trip west. Every day for seven more school days I'll put obstacles in your path. There are rivers to cross, mountains to climb, stampedes to avoid, hailstorms, perhaps snakes. Starting tomorrow, you'll have to deal with them on your own."

Clyde lay flat on his back and looked out the window. The wind was now blowing swirls of snow. Some of it stuck to the glass, melted, and slid down in icy rivers.

"We might not be here tomorrow," he said. "It might be a snow day, and then school will be closed and we'll all be home watching TV."

Meg walked over and shut the blinds. "That's a real blizzard out there," she said. "But for you, here and now, it is March 15, 1846. You're settled in for the night in a field just outside of Independence, Missouri."

She flicked the lights off. With the blinds closed, the room was as dark as twilight.

"Oooooooo," Clyde said. "I'm scared."

"Oooooooo," murmured Jessica.

"Grow up," Orin told them.

"And scoot in closer," Meg said. "You're sitting around a bonfire, both to keep you warm in the early spring chill and to shed light in the overcast night. You need to talk. You're gathered here for a serious purpose."

"My father thinks this isn't serious,"

Clyde said loudly, moving back from the circle. "He says we should stick to Reading, Writing, and Arithmetic in school."

"My mother thinks so, too," Jessica told him. "She says exactly the same thing."

"There'll be light frost tonight," Meg went on, as if they hadn't spoken, "but you don't mind. You're warm and you're safe. You've corralled your livestock, and your children are all tucked in, almost asleep."

Her voice was low and soft. It was hard *not* to listen.

Dinah took a deep breath and leaned toward the imaginary fire.

"In March the ground is still soggy from the winter thaw and the spring rains," Meg went on. "If you took your covered wagons out this month, the wheels would bog down in the mud. Also, the prairie grass is still just shoots, not quite high enough for your animals to eat well along the way. Tomorrow, WOW time, will be April 15, 1846, and that's when you will leave Independence."

"What do we do tonight?" Michael asked

her. "We already got our supplies and all."

"Yes, I have a copy of the supplies you chose. Actually, this is a big night for you, Hiram," Meg said, calling him by the name on his tag. "Tonight you must choose your wagon-train leader and put together a charter—rules to live by on the trail."

"This is so bogus," said Marilou, sitting up on her knees and bouncing on her heels. "Turn the lights back on. What do we need a leader for, anyway? Why don't we just *go* and get it over with."

"I hate rules," Clyde said.

"First, pick your leader," Meg told them. "Your leader has the final say, makes all the hard decisions. You have to choose carefully. Remember, in this room, you are not fifth graders, you are adults with families who depend on you. You have a new set of problems, and you need to have rules to solve them by."

Nobody said anything. Dinah put her hands out to warm them by the campfire. "Okay," she said finally, "let's do it. Anybody want to be leader?"

"Meg," Sarah called. "Time out. Does it have to be a guy?"

"Okay. One time out," Meg said. "It would certainly have been a man in 1846. But you can pick anybody. Just remember, your lives are in his hands."

"Or hers," Sarah said.

"Or hers."

Marilou stood up. "Just to get this over with, I'll volunteer to be leader. Everybody who wants me, Hepsibah Winchester, to lead them west, raise their hands."

Nobody did.

"Nice try. Anybody else want to be in charge?" Dinah asked.

"Wait a minute," Marilou wailed. "What's wrong with me?"

"You didn't get any votes, is all," Dinah said. "Who else..."

"Hold on," Orin interrupted her. "That's not fair. What have you accomplished, Hepsibah Winchester, that would make you right for the job? Tell us about you."

"That's better. Well, I'm really, really good at giving directions. It said on that sheet that I lived on this farm in Pennsylvania. We had to leave because we owed everybody and his brother. We've got two little girls. The oldest one's seven. And that's it. All in favor of me say aye."

"Aye," Michael said. Marilou tossed her hair and smiled at him.

"Sure," Sarah told Zach. "Like I'd let her boss me around."

"So, you got one vote," Dinah said. "I'm sorry, Marilou, but you lose."

"How come you're running this, anyway?" Marilou asked her. "If Brandi and Tiffani were here..."

"I'm just doing it because nobody else was. I nominate Orin. He's very smart, and that's why."

Nobody else thought so, so Orin just shrugged and shook his head at her.

Dinah looked around the room. "Jane, how about you or your fine husband, Ernest."

"I'll think it over," Clyde said.

Jessica just looked at the ceiling.

"You better think fast," Dinah told him.

She waited a beat. "Going, going,...gone."

"I'll do it if you want me to," Michael said. "I never led a wagon train before, but I'm a farmer and they know about cattle and weather and hard times."

"Anybody got a question for Hiram?" Dinah asked.

"What would you do if everybody wanted to break up and go in different directions?" Zach tried.

Michael took a deep breath. "I'd tell them that now we're like this big family helping each other, but if they cut out on their own nobody would be there if they got sick or lost. They'd probably die. We have to stick together." He grinned. "How's that?"

"What would you do if I discovered gold and made you all my miners?" Clyde asked, like that was some question.

"If you want to be leader, say so now before we vote," Dinah said.

Clyde shrugged and crossed his arms. "Who made *her* boss?"

Dinah's legs were killing her. Both feet were fast asleep.

"All in favor of Hiram Winchester, stand up," she said, and she stood up. Way up.

Marilou hugged Michael and popped up. His face turned purple. "So what, he's my husband," she told the group.

Slowly, everyone stood. Everyone but Jessica and Clyde. They sat still and crossed their arms.

"Six standing for Hiram," Dinah said. "Two in the grass. Hiram's our leader."

"Okay, what about rules?" the new leader asked after everyone else had sat down. "I say murderers should be banished."

"Murderers should be shot," Clyde said loudly. "Cattle rustlers should be banished. We send cattle rustlers home without bread and water."

"Anybody getting this down?" Michael asked. "Marilou, will you write this down? Then we'll all sign it."

"Bummer." Marilou gave a heavy sigh but grabbed a pencil and wrote.

"What about plain old thieves?" Sarah asked.

"You get a whipping."

"Three whips."

"Ten lashes."

Clyde waved his hand. "For stealing you should get your hand chopped off."

"Wouldn't it make sense," interrupted Orin, "that when there's a problem, we vote and the majority rules? I mean, then we don't have to decide every crime and punishment right now. Maybe they won't happen."

They all looked at Meg, who smiled and nodded.

"Lookout guards. We've got to have those every night and everybody's got to take turns, women, too," Sarah said. "Okay?"

"What if one person shoots a deer? Who gets to eat it?" Dinah asked.

"The guy who shoots it shares the meat," Michael said. "But his family gets to keep the skin. How about that? Raise your hands if that's okay."

Everyone's hand went up except Clyde's and Jessica's.

"Members of the train should try to keep peace with each other."

"*Must* try," Michael said.

"Time's just about running out," Meg told them. "You can add to the contract when you need to."

The lights flicked on.

"You know," Orin told Dinah, "all that time you were talking, your little brother Buster was standing behind you making incredible Silly Putty faces. He'll be the clown of the wagon train."

Dinah almost stuck out her tongue and crossed her eyes, but she didn't. "He's got to do something," she said. "He's short for his age."

"Wagon Train Seven, that wasn't bad," Meg told them. "Maybe you didn't ask quite enough questions of your leader, but you thought well. And most of you took part in writing the contract. The rest of you will have to urge Ernest and Jane to join in more seriously next time. I'm giving you fifteen points out of twenty."

"We're getting *grades*?" Jessica shouted. "No fair. Nobody *said*."

"You're graded on Math and Science

and your journals. Why not here? In fact, the number of total points you lose on the trail will be important to you. For every twenty points you lose, you have to go through a mountain pass at the end of your journey next Thursday. At each mountain pass, you must throw a die."

"A *die*?" Clyde asked.

"Singular for dice," Orin explained. "One dice is a die."

"Right. And if you throw a six on the pass," Meg went on, "you are automatically lost in an avalanche."

"So we, like, die?"

"Basically, yes. And every extra time you have to throw increases your chances of losing."

"So, what does that mean? We die?" Zach asked.

"It means your characters don't reach Oregon. You'll go to the big Friday breakfast and square dance as people who already live in Oregon."

"Big deal," Clyde said. "Big fat deal."

"Fat deal," said Jessica.

"Meanwhile," Meg went on, "tomorrow afternoon, you move off toward Kansas. I promise sunny skies."

Dinah sighed. "We'll do okay."

"And deep water," Meg went on. "Deep and wide."

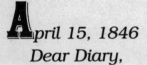 **Dear Diary**

April 15, 1846

Dear Diary,

You remember how mad I was at first about coming West? I still am. I would have been happy milking cows in Ohio forever if we hadn't owed so much money. It was awful that my really, really best friends in the world went with somebody else. We would have had a good time no matter what.

But I got stuck in this skunky wagon train with the short dork and the tall clown. It turns out that the short dork is a rich doctor who's got lots of cattle. He keeps curing people's blisters and dysentery. He won't let anybody drink their Moore's Super Elixir. I think that's stupid. I paid big money for it. I think he's a quack.

The tall clown, whose name is now Lydia, tried to take over last month. She wouldn't let me get elected wagon-train leader. We showed her, though. We elected my husband Hiram.

That would have been good, but we've had problems.

At first we were going along fine and then we ran into this river, the Wakarusa. It had these really, really steep banks. We talked about what to do. Big-deal Lydia said what if she got on their horse and looked for a better place to cross. My husband, the leader, said, sure, why not.

Some people wanted to take the wheels off the wagons and slide them down the riverbanks like sleds. Some people said we should tie ropes to the back of each wagon. Then we could all hold on to the ropes and slow the wagon as it went down so it wouldn't crash. We decided that taking the wheels off would be a pain, so we did the rope thing. It took _forever_, and somebody's pretend brother had to go and get a broken leg. We were in mud up to our knees. The hogs on the farm at home were better off than us.

Of course, when Lydia came back, Meg had her say how she'd found a place three miles down where the banks weren't steep at all. Everybody got really, really mad at Hiram because he didn't wait for her report before starting down the bank.

I, personally, wasn't mad at him. Just everybody else.

Then, we got hungry. We wanted to build a fire, but Meg said there wasn't any wood. So we went out to find fuel. The stuff we had to find was gross. The women, even me, had to gather up buffalo chips in our aprons. Do you know what that is?! We lit the so-called chips in a pit the guys dug about eight inches wide and a foot deep. Then we set skillets over the fire and cooked our beans and chicken. _We burned_ _that stuff to cook food over._ It was disgusting.

I wouldn't eat the chicken. Remember that cage of chickens we strapped to the side of our wagon? Well, before you can cook them you have to wring their necks so their heads come off, then you have to dip them in boiling water, and then you've got to pull out all their feathers. All that just for drumsticks you're going to cook over buffalo plop.

My little girls hate this trip. They cry, and Meg says the littlest one has a fever. She drank some gunky green water is why. She throws up and has chills and she's thirsty. The doctor has me give her milk, but she can't keep it down.

I wish we'd stayed home.

Hepsibah Winchester

May 15, 1846
Dear Diary,
I walked eight miles today. I thought I'd be riding in the wagon, but it's so bumpy

what with the ruts and the prairie-dog holes that it could knock your teeth out. My husband Martin is a doctor and he won't let me ride much because he says it's not good for the baby.

This land is brown and flat. It's Kansas. It's a place to get out of. There aren't any trees. There's no place to hide.

Three nights ago we wanted to hide so bad. It was after midnight when the lightning started. Meg did this by flipping the lights in Ms. Stefanik's room off and on and off and on. It was cool. And then there were wild winds that whipped some tents off their pegs and up into the sky. The hail the wind blew in was as big as hen's eggs. It rained hard all night and the water dripped right through the wagon cover. All of the children cried, all except my amazing little brother Buster. He told jokes and made us laugh. I think he's going to grow up to be president of the United States.

But he couldn't stop the rain. All my sugar got dissolved. My flour was totally soaked—we had to throw it out. All that food wasted. Martin lost four head of cattle in the stampede.

Next day when the train tried to start out, the wagon wheels sank down in the mud, especially ours, since we've got that pump organ. Even though he hasn't played it yet, Martin says he just won't leave it behind.

Two days and nights we waited for the ground to dry out enough so we could push on. Buster made a full-sized mud sculpture of Barney Bilkum holding a bottle of elixir in each hand. Everybody loves little Buster.

I can feel the baby move inside me. I'm scared.

Love,
Lydia

June 15, 1846
Dear Diary,
We forded the Platte River, a mile wide and, after the rains, four feet deep in some places.

The mosquitoes are a veritable plague.

What can a doctor do about mosquitoes? And the drinking water is cholera bearing. I want to tell them to boil it first to kill the germs, but I'm not supposed to know about that in 1846. It would be such an easy thing to do. The older Winchester girl has a high fever now. I hope we don't lose her.

If she's up to it, she'll have buffalo meat tonight with the rest of us. We spotted a big herd of them last week and all the men rode off to shoot supper and to get a skin or two against the cold.

We all shot at about the same time, so it's hard to tell who made the hits, but we harvested two. Then we dragged them back, skinned them, and salted the meat to preserve it. Johann claimed he'd gotten them both, but I reminded him that he hadn't even raised his arms to shoot. In the end we decided just to share the meat and the skins. Johann was angry and refused to help.

The hardest news is last. Two men were on watch last night, keeping the cattle corralled. First they saw something move.

Then they heard whistling sounds like those a bird makes. Meg told them they couldn't see what it was in the dark, but Johann said he was sure it was an Indian attack and he bet there were thousands of them out there and we'd all be scalped. He told Hiram that as leader he had to do something and do it fast. Hiram did. He shot his gun straight at the noise. He just lifted his hands and went, "Pow-pow-pow!"

That scared us. And we were right to be. The next morning when we were packing up to move on, a big group of angry Shawnees (actually Meg) came and told us that during the night one of their men had been shot near our camp.

Hiram often jokes about things, but he couldn't make this funny. He told them he thought he was shooting at a pig-eating bird. That was a lie, though, and they knew it. Hepsibah told them we were really, really sorry, but they said that wasn't enough. They demanded two of our children to take the injured man's place. The bullet had blown his kneecap all the way off. He'd never be able to walk again. The whole wagon train got together to decide what to do.

Jane and Ernest didn't offer any of their five children, but they said the Indians could have Buster any day because he's such a pest and show-off. Lydia was outraged. She made Buster run away to our wagon and hide behind my pump organ.

We told the Indians we wouldn't give them any children. They said we had to. They said they didn't know if they could prevent their people from seeking retribution if we didn't. We had harmed one of their men. Johann said they weren't getting anything from him.

Hepsibah asked them if they'd take a horse instead, but that was easy for her to say because the Winchesters don't have a horse.

They said for six horses they would call it even.

Hiram said one horse, take it or leave it.

Apparently Buster had crept back to

listen, because one of the Indians found him. When they asked Hepsibah for her children, too, Hiram raised his gun again.

Lydia stepped up and told the head Indian we only had four horses. And that was true.

In the end, we voted six to two to let them take three horses. Clara and Johann were mad that they had to give up anything to get Buster back. But it wasn't just Buster. The horses were to make up for shooting the man, too. The Shawnees said one man is worth a lot more than three horses, and I guess that's true.

Hiram felt bad about the shooting. He said he didn't like being wagon train leader. It made him, he said, feel stupid. He quit, and he wouldn't change his mind.

I don't know what we'll do. Meg won't tell us. She only gave us a twelve out of twenty today. We argued a lot. As Hepsibah would say, "Bummer."

Respectfully,
Martin Jones, M.D.
("Big Marty")

8

☞Ambush

"**W**ait up!"

That wouldn't be hard. Dinah wasn't exactly jogging. She was, in fact, slogging home from school through thick wet drifts of snow. Chunks of it were stuck to her jeans and caked between her socks and her untied sneakers. Icy water soaked all the way down to her toes.

She stopped to look back.

"Wait up!" the voice called again.

"Is that you under all that stuff?" Dinah asked. She knew the eyes. It was Orin, almost running.

He was huffing. "Sorry, but my mother says...my mother insists...that I bundle up in the snow and stay dry. I catch colds...catch colds very, very easily."

"I don't see how a cold could *find* you in there, much less catch you. I hate to tell you this, but when it's not below zero, only bank robbers wear ski masks."

She scooped up a handful of snow, looked for a neckhole to drop it in, and, not finding one, plopped it down on top of his yellow cap.

He shook his head like a wet puppy.

"I'll just run ahead," Dinah said, "so the police won't think I'm your bandit buddy." She took two dinosaur steps.

"Wait up!" he called.

She stopped. "I don't want to wait. It's Friday afternoon and Kaat's coming over. We're going to have hot cocoa with big fat marshmallows. Anyway, my toes are freezing. Don't those boots hurt your knees?"

"Rubber boots keep dampness *out*," he explained patiently. "Sneakers, even your fine black canvas high-tops, soak water *in.* It's a law of nature. That's why your feet are cold and mine are not. And, tell me, why is your head bare? You want to wear one of my scarves?"

"But then you'd only have three, and the cold might catch... Wait a minute." Dinah stopped again. "Are you trying to save me from the flu so I can pull your covered wagon out of the Oregon mud? If so, forget it, because I may just go to California instead and become the first Hollywood star."

"Don't even think about it. Don't leave me, Lydia," he said. "Don't abandon me in the Great Wide West. Stay. If not for me, then for Buster's sake."

Dinah laughed. She liked him as Dr. Martin Jones, but he was pretty funny as Orin Philpot, too. He waddled toward her, skidded, windmilled his arms, and fell into a snowbank, flat on his back.

She laughed again, harder. "You look like a belly-up turtle."

He lay there, flapping. "Be a good soul

and help me up. Please. I must have stepped on a slick spot."

Dinah shook her head. Dr. Martin Jones could cure a whole caravan. Orin Philpot couldn't even walk home from school without help. She turned so he wouldn't see her smile. Let him figure it out. It would be, as Mr. Marconi liked to say, a learning experience.

Thunk! A snowball smacked the back of her head. Hard. A clump of it caught in her hair.

Orin? On the attack? Amazing. Dinah reached down, packed a quick ball, and was just about to turn and take aim when—*Pow!*—another one clipped her on the ear.

She wound up, spun around, flung the wad of snow, and got Orin square on the nose, the only skin she could see.

"Cut it out," he called. "I didn't do it. I couldn't have, even if I'd wanted to."

It was true. He was still on the ground, trying to flop belly down.

Thwack! Wham! Splat! That sure wasn't

Orin. Great balls of snow were pelting Dinah from everywhere but him.

Then the army marched out from a clump of pines, still throwing. Clyde, Zach, and Michael. They'd been waiting, building up a pile of ammunition.

"Who is that masked man?" Michael called. He heaved a wad of snow at Orin. Direct hit.

"Ambush!" Orin yelled. "We've been ambushed. Let's work this out. You want our horses? They're Arabians. Very fast. Very valuable. How about our matched pair of creamy white oxen? They're yours. We surrender."

Dinah ran back and pulled Orin up. "We do not," she said. "They attacked us. Come on. Take off those mittens and start packing."

Bam! Whump! Blowie! It was a snowball blitz. The three guys didn't have to stop and reload. They'd built up a supply.

Dinah made a few good hits. She got Zach on the chin. But Orin only threw fistfuls of snow, powdering the enemy.

Some of it sprinkled Clyde, who got him right back with a hard ball. "If I had a white handkerchief I'd wave it," Orin told Dinah.

"Terrific. They'd get your germs and run away spitting up yellow gunk. Serve them right, too."

At the end, Dinah and Orin both looked like Frosty the Snowkids, one tall and skinny, the other short and stout.

Michael came out juggling the last three balls. "Sorry about that," he told them. "We just got tired of waiting for Marilou. Then you came along."

"And for Brandi and Tiffani," Zach said. "They must have gone another way."

"Good thing, too," Clyde said. "*They'd* probably have murdered us." He thwacked Orin on the back and a layer of snow fell off his front.

"All of life is just a matter of timing," Orin told him.

"Couldn't let that good snow go to waste. Perfect packing," Zach said. "You two still married?"

"Cut it out." Dinah edged away from Orin. "This isn't Kansas."

"Mr. and Mrs. Know-It-All," Clyde said.

"You forget, we're on your side," Orin told him. "Aren't we in this wagon train together? All for one? One for all?"

"Not exactly," Clyde said. He packed up an extra-hard ball.

"If you're not for us, you're agin us," Orin told him.

"Right," Clyde said. "That's right. Agin you. That's what I am. And I've got an idea what to do about it, too." He whispered something in Zach's ear and laughed. "What do you think?"

Zach shook his head. "That's dumb."

"You're no fun," Clyde said. "I'm going to do it."

"Do what?" Dinah asked him.

Clyde grinned a small, mean grin. "That's for me to know and..."

"Do we get to play Twenty Questions?" Orin asked.

"It's a secret," Clyde said. "Want to guess?"

"If it's a secret, you should certainly keep it," Orin told him.

"You get on my nerves, you know that?" Clyde said. "I'd be careful if I were you." He packed the snowball harder aimed it at Orin, and then, all at once, dropped it and crossed his arms.

"Mr. Marconi's driving by," he whispered. "Everybody smile." Snowball fights on the way home were strictly forbidden. School rules. Mr. Marconi had warned them just before the bell, "A three-page essay on Kindness to Others for snowball fighters."

Mr. Marconi slowed down and opened his car window. "How you doing?" he asked.

"We're doing snow angels," Dinah called to him. "You know," and she flapped her arms wide.

Mr. Marconi waved and drove on.

"His secret's about WOW," Zach told them, "and it's..."

"Hey, no fair telling." Clyde kicked at a snowbank.

"Oh, I know what it is," Orin said.

"Beneath all that hostility he thinks WOW is wonderful. And just now he was trying to do me in so he could run away across the open prairie with my beloved Lydia, with whom he is madly in love."

"Sure, right," Clyde said.

"But I won't let you, sir. No, never." Orin grinned.

So did Dinah.

"You think you're so smart," Clyde said. "My dad's always bugging me about grades, but I tell him it's only freaks like you that get good grades. School is for dorks. But I've figured it out, all right, and after Monday, the shrimp-dork and the dino-clown won't think they're so great anymore."

"Wait a minute," said Dinah. "Us? You're talking about Orin and me? You think *we* think we're great?"

"You, you're always standing up and giving orders, and Meg lets you get away with it because she's sorry for you or something. And Orin, he uses big words like we're all stupid and he's not."

"Well, I'm not," Orin told him.

"You know what Mr. Marconi said," Clyde went on. "He said a lot more of those guys got killed by each other than by Indians."

"You're going to *kill* us?" Orin asked.

"Nobody's going to kill anybody," Michael told them. "Or shoot their kneecaps, either. That was so dumb of me."

"I'm out of here." Dinah turned and sprinted off.

Orin followed as fast as his bulk would let him. "Meg doesn't...." he called after her. "Meg doesn't feel....."

She slowed so he could catch up.

"Meg doesn't feel sorry for you. Clyde's just..." He caught his breath.

"You shouldn't bug him. You're too little."

"He asks for it. Besides, I've got you to protect me."

Dinah shivered.

Orin unwound one of his scarves and gave it to her.

She wrapped it around her neck. "I

think I really will stay home Monday," she said. "He can tease me all he wants to, but I won't let him be mean to Lydia."

"Well, that's bizarre. She's fake and you're real."

She pulled the scarf tighter.

"Think about it," said Orin, lifting the mask off his face. "Whatever he does, you can just cross your eyes at him like a pioneer dinosaur. It's always worked before."

"Lydia doesn't make faces. She's nice. And he's wrong. She's not bossy. She's smart and strong."

"She's no better than you are. The only difference is that you *help* him make fun of you."

Dinah rubbed her ears, then cupped her hands over them. "I've got an earache. I'll stay home."

"You won't have an earache Monday. Besides, that's one day you've got to be there," Orin told her. "It's a big day. Did you forget? Monday is July. You're going to have a baby."

Dirty Dishwater

Dinah watched as Orin waddled away through swirls of snow. She pulled his scarf up higher, stepped carefully across a patch of black ice at the curb, then trudged on with her head down, turning the corner onto Maple Street. Three more blocks and she'd be home.

Friday. Nanna would be there, baby-sitting Boris. Her mom and dad were in Florida with Grandma Gardiner for a whole week, so Boris would be cranky.

But Kaat would come over. First they'd drink mugs of hot cocoa, then they'd find something good to do. They always did.

"It's his. I know it is," she heard behind her. "I saw him twist it on this afternoon. It's the only yuck-green scarf with yellow polka dots I ever saw."

"He got it from his grandfather. I asked him once, it looked so weird."

"But that's not him wearing it."

"Not unless he really, really stretched."

"And turned his hair dirty dishwater blond."

"But if it isn't little Orin wearing his cute green scarf, then who could it *be*?"

As if they didn't know. They knew all right. The three girls in back of Dinah laughed. Very funny. Even without looking she knew who they were. Marilou, Brandi, and Tiffani.

"Him so tall and her so small, they look cute together, don't you think?" Brandi said.

She could turn and make a Jurassic face. She could dino-walk back and say something roll-on-the-ground funny. But packing words wasn't as easy as packing snow. So she just raised her feet high to clear the drifts, and ran.

Since looking back would mean she cared, she kept her eyes on the path. But if the girls were still behind her, they'd stopped talking, and since they never stopped talking, they must have turned down Fourth Street toward Marilou's house.

After a block, she slipped inside Moderne Cleaners on the corner and glanced down the street. They were gone. She took a deep breath. Kaat would just have to wait while her nose thawed. But the steam from the shirt pressers didn't warm her. She cooled the store instead.

Her reflection in the cleaner's mirror was staring back at her hair. So that's what color it was. Dirty dishwater.

"Funnygirl Dinah Barnes loses out on the Oscar once more, folks," the emcee would say. "Could it be those curls that remind one of—sink suds?"

She covered her hair and her ears with

the scarf of yuck green, pulled it tight, and ran all the way home.

"Hi, Dinahbear," her grandmother called when she got there. "Your friend just phoned. She'll be here in ten minutes." Then she looked at Dinah's feet. "Oh, my goodness, your shoes are soaked. Don't children wear boots anymore?"

"Hi, Nan. Only dorks do."

Dinah kicked off her shoes, uncoiled the scarf, and dropped it with her coat on a bench by the door.

"Dry dorks, I expect. You missed your mom's call by five minutes. All's well. She sends their love and said not to tell you that it hit eighty degrees in Miami."

"Eighty degrees? Wow! I bet snowball fights are a mess down there." Dinah blew on her fingers. "Is the cocoa hot? Or should I make some?"

"Oh, we're out of cocoa. I made Kool-Aid instead. Boris insisted."

"Kool-Aid! But it's January. Kool-Aid is July."

"It was on sale at Meat & Shoppe. Five

packages for a dollar. We bought ten. Boris begged so."

"Well, maybe I could nuke it. How would it be hot with marshmallows?"

"Careful, sweetie," Nanna warned. Boris was chugging out of the kitchen pushing a small dump truck loaded with a small glass of red juice.

"Look at me, Dinah." He raced the truck faster.

"Don't spill," Nanna told him.

"You are a potty," he said.

She smiled. "Now, now."

"You can't let him get away with that," Dinah told her. "Hi, there, Buster."

"I am not Buster. You call me Buster and you are a big number two." He sped his cargo down the hall, "Chug, chug," sloshing a trail of red behind him.

"He shouldn't talk so gross," Dinah said. "He's just a baby."

"That's why he does it. He's just four. When you're four you're interested in the toilet. He'll get over it. Besides, he misses his mother, poor dear."

"He's getting red spots on Mom's tan rug," Dinah said. "I'll go get bleach or something."

"No, no, don't you worry. It'll come right out."

Dinah's toes still tingled with the cold. "Okay, then, I'll take a shower before Kaat comes. We had a sandstorm on the prairie today."

In the shower she closed her eyes, thought Florida, and felt like a day at the beach. Then she dried herself off with a Big Bird towel. After pulling on a cozy old sweatshirt and sweatpants, she wiped the steam off the medicine-chest mirror with her sleeve. Little rivers were dripping down her neck and off her nose.

She didn't put Big Bird to work on her hair, just watched as the water ran off the strands. "Bathwater beige," she thought.

"Knock, knock," Kaat called from the other side of the door. "You trying for first in the Clean Kid Contest or what? I've been here for hours."

"Not true," Dinah said as she opened

the door. "Two minutes tops. What's that yellow stuff?"

Kaat clinked the ice-cubes in her glass. "Nice cold Kool-Aid. Your brother says it's scrumptious. Want a sip?"

Dinah tasted it and made a face. "I thought he was drinking the red kind."

"This is new. He spilled the other. He said it was bug blood. But he and your grandmother are sopping it up with paper towels. She gave us a plate of fig bars and said to stay out of the kitchen until the floor's dry. The cookies are frozen, okay?"

"I'm so starved, I could eat them grilled over buffalo chips."

Kaat laughed as they settled on the rug in Dinah's room. "It's been a funny day. We had a blast in WOW. Did you?" She took a big circle of red string from her jeans pocket and stretched it between her hands.

Dinah shook her head. "A blast wouldn't cover it. What're you making?" She watched as Kaat looped the string through her fingers.

"Guess." Kaat shifted the yarn quickly front to back, over and under. Her hands were like dancers. Then suddenly there it was.

"A butterfly." Dinah touched the wings. "I wish I could do that, but my fingers move like carrots. String just stays string for me."

"All you need is practice. We'll do one together. Okay? You do a cat's cradle and then we'll make diamonds from it."

She handed the string to Dinah, who started slowly, with Kaat once again explaining how to loop and hook it with her fingers.

"Say, have you tried dipping your fig bar in Kool-Aid?" Kaat asked.

"No."

"Don't. It's gross." Kaat began to pinch and pull and catch the string stretched between Dinah's hands, telling her what to do next and next. When Kaat finally let go, Dinah held a criss-cross of diamonds in her hands.

"Amazing," Dinah said. She picked up a cookie without taking the string from her fingers and began to munch on it.

"Did you guys make a shelter today?" Kaat asked. "To keep the sandstorm out?"

Dinah nodded, her mouth full.

"So, you know how Mr. Marconi gave us newspapers and tape to build with? Well, my husband Charles, who is so cute...well, he figures out this way to fold and tape and prop everything up. I can see it won't work. I know it won't work, and I say it won't work. I'm sure it won't work, but we build it anyway. And guess what?"

"It doesn't work." Dinah said.

"Right." They both laughed.

"But when all ten of us finally get under it, Mr. Marconi says he's the sandstorm. And he blows—I mean just *blows,* not huff-and-puff stuff the way the big bad wolf trashes the pigs or anything—and the whole tent collapses on top of us. And we all roll around in the paper and tape and laugh and laugh and laugh. Especially Charles."

"So, what did Mr. Marconi do?"

"He laughed hardest." The diamonds in

Dinah's hands were tangled now. Kaat took the yarn and began to flick and pull it into new shapes. "By the way, your hair is dripping," she said.

Dinah blotted her bangs on her sleeve. "Marilou and Tiffani and Brandi walked behind me on the way home. They said my hair is the color of dirty dishwater. Do you think so? True, now."

"Mmmmmmmmmmm."

"What's that supposed to mean?"

"That means I've made a mistake and this string is never going to turn into a porcupine."

"But what about my hair?"

Kaat dropped the string, leaned back against a chair and looked. "It sure is as *wet* as dishwater. Aren't you really, really, *really* flattered, though, that Marilou took the time to think about your hair instead of hers?" She grinned. "You know, I saw this article about hair a couple of months ago. It was in the Kids News in the *Tribune.*"

"Let me guess." Dinah pulled a long

strand down to the tip of her nose. "It said it's not what your hair is like that counts, it's what you're like *inside* that matters. Right?"

"No, actually, it said you could dye your hair with Kool-Aid."

"It did not."

"Cross my heart."

"Did you try it?"

"We only had orange-pineapple, and all that did was make my hair smell funny. I don't think it works on black."

"But on dishwater blond?"

"Maybe." Kaat held up her glass. "You could try this, but it's got ice cubes in it."

"Lemon-yellow hair. I don't think so," Dinah said.

Kaat leaned forward and eyed her. "Why not? Just for fun. It's Friday. Your grandmother says it comes right out."

"Yellow? Forget it."

"Haven't you always wondered how you'd look as Goldilocks?"

"Never. And whoever heard of a lemon-headed dinosaur?"

"Stop that," Kaat said. "Tell you what. I'll tiptoe over the wet kitchen floor and see if I can find some magic yellow potion. Meet you in the bathroom."

Great Green Gobs

Kaat kicked the bathroom door shut with her stockinged foot. She was holding the glass pitcher with both hands. "There's only about an inch left of the second batch," she told Dinah. "I think they're freezing some of it as ice cubes. Okay, hold your head way down in the sink and I'll pour."

"Let's talk about this," Dinah said.

"Okay. I can only stay about half an hour more. We could go outside and build us a nice quick shelter out of newspapers and tape in case there's an early evening sandstorm—or you could put your head in the sink."

Dinah put her head in the sink. "This is crazy."

Almost at once she felt a cold trickle down her scalp and watched streams of yellow snaking toward the drain.

"It's not working," Kaat told her. "Your hair's barely turning."

"My eyes sting."

"Keep them shut. And wait a second. I brought another whole package just in case." She tore it open and dumped the crystals on Dinah's hair. "Oh, wow."

"Oh, wow, what?" Dinah asked.

"Ow, wow, I guess all the packages of Kool-Aid on the kitchen table weren't yellow. But don't worry, it'll come right out."

Dinah raised her head, opened her eyes a slit, and looked in the mirror. She blinked. Twice. Around the edges, her hair looked like it had before, but the top part did not. It was different. It was *green*.

"I don't believe this," she said. Then she sniffed. "What flavor is it?"

"Stick your head under the faucet and we'll wash it out. I'm sorry. I thought they were all lemon. Hurry."

"But what's the flavor?" Dinah asked. She stuck her tongue out to lick a stream of it. The green was spreading.

Kaat held the label up to the light. "It says, 'Add water to watch the powder color change into...Great Bluedini.' I guess your hair is Lemon plus Great Bluedini. I'm really sorry."

"Great Bluedini!" Dinah giggled. She started to rub the powder in as if it were shampoo. The warm, melting Kool-Aid streamed through her hair and down her face. She laughed harder and rubbed faster. It splattered. It flecked the fogging mirror. It sprayed Kaat, who squealed. There were green spots on the bathroom wall.

They could not stop laughing.

Chunks of unmelted powder clung to Dinah's hair. She broke them up with her fingers and pulled them straight out from her scalp, through to the tips of her curls.

Kaat sat down on the toilet seat and held her sides.

"Di-nah," a small voice wailed outside the door. "I gotta go. You been in there a long time. I gotta pee."

"Let's wash...let's wash it out now," Kaat said, gasping. Tears were streaming down her face, she'd laughed so hard.

"It said in the *newspaper* to do this?" Dinah asked. "What was the article about, anyway?"

"'Halloween Costumes, Cheap and Easy.'"

"Boooooooo. I am zee green ghost. I am," Dinah said grandly, "zee Great Bluedini." As she raised her hands to cast a spell she looked at them. And then she looked at them again. "My fingers. Kaat, they're...."

"Greenish," Kaat said. "Bluish green. They look like aquamarine crayons. This is too weird. Let's wash it out."

"Dinah!" Boris began to kick the door. "If I wet my pants, it's all your fault. I'll tell Mom."

"Okay, okay." Training Boris had not been easy. Dinah wrapped the Big Bird towel around her head, opened the door, and let him in.

"It smells in here," he said.

"Lemon-blueberry surprise," Kaat told him. They both fled to Dinah's room and slammed the door.

It took Boris about thirty seconds. "Nan-na!" he wailed. "Nan-na! I wet my pants. And Kool-Aid is all over the bathroom. Dinah did it."

"What'll she do?" Kaat asked. "She won't be mad, will she?" What'll *we* do?"

"I don't know what I'm going to do. But I know what you've got to do. Look out the window," Dinah told her. "It's almost dark. You better start home. I'll just rinse this out and then Nanna and I will have a big laugh...or something."

"You certain? I should help you clean up the bathroom, at least. It's my fault."

"No it isn't. I made the mess." Dinah pulled the towel tighter around her head. Then she handed Kaat her coat. "If you

111

hurry home you won't get in trouble. And if I work fast, neither will I."

Kaat closed the front door quietly when she left, but when Dinah reached the bathroom, her grandmother was standing outside it, waiting. The white tiles, the sink, and the floor were all spattered blue and yellow and green. She couldn't pretend nothing had happened.

So Dinah unwound the towel.

Nanna caught her breath. "That's a wig, isn't it," she said. "One of those clown wigs."

"It's that bad?" Dinah asked. "It's okay. The color is pure Kool-Aid. That's all. Don't worry. It'll come right out, like you said."

"Are you Dinah?" Boris asked.

"Oh, my. Oh, dear. Oh, good grief. I know I said it would come out of the *rug*. But in fact it hasn't. I've tried, but it hasn't." She glanced over Dinah's shoulder. "Where's your friend?"

"She left. It was time. Her mother wants her home by dark."

"Did she make you do it?"

"Of course not. I did it because I'm eleven. If Boris can do stuff because he's four, I can do stuff because I'm eleven."

"You *sound* like Dinah," Boris said.

"Eleven's old enough to know better. Your mother will never let me baby-sit again."

"You're her mother-in-law. She can't fire you."

"You're beautiful," Boris told Dinah, and hugged her knees.

"I'm afraid you look like a leprechaun," said Nanna.

"Leprechauns are *little* people," Dinah told her. Then she turned the water on in the shower. "Don't worry, I'll make it go away."

"You're green, you know that?" Boris asked her. "Like on TV. You're the Jolly Green Giant."

"You scrub hard now," her grandmother said as Dinah closed the door.

"Don't worry," Dinah called back, staring in the mirror. Her hair was the color of Orin's scarf. Yuck green. And her cheeks were striped. She wiggled her turquoise fingers. Boris had it right. She was the Jolly Green Giant.

But Kaat was gone and there was nobody to ho-ho-ho with. Besides, it wasn't funny anymore. She stuck out her bottom lip and her eyes began to fill with tears.

"Scrub *extra* hard," her grandmother called through the door. "You can't go to school looking like that. You hear?"

She heard. She'd scrub. Lydia would never have yuck-green hair.

Under the shower, she poured on shampoo, thinking, You can't go to school like that. The shower smelled of hot, soapy Kool-Aid, without marshmallows.

But when she stepped out and checked the mirror once more, the color was still there. The green had not washed down the drain.

With the water off she could hear Boris singing on the other side of the door, "Bea-u-ti-ful Di-nah."

You *absolutely* can't go to school like that, she thought.

She smiled at the mirror. Then I won't. That's it. Nobody's going to tease Lydia about her hair or anything else. She won't be there. I can't go to school Monday. My grandmother won't let me.

And then she began to laugh.

The green giant was jolly again.

This Wagon Train Is in Big Trouble

"**H**ave you seen Dinah this morning?" Kaat asked Sarah.

"I don't think so," Sarah told her. "I don't remember."

"Settle down, class," Mr. Marconi called out. "Miles to go before you sleep today."

"If you'd seen her," Kaat said, "you'd have remembered. Trust me on that." She hurried off to sit with her wagon train.

"Dinah Barnes?" Mr. Marconi called. "Where is our fine Mrs. Jones this splendid Monday morning?"

"I bet she skips," Clyde whispered to

Zach. "I just bet. Can't take the heat. But I can still turn it on. The Shrimp's here." He grinned.

Orin, hearing him, smiled and waved.

Sarah tapped Orin on the head with her ruler. "Looks like your wife left you," she teased. "Too bad. You'll have to cook the cactus-and-rattlesnake soup all by yourself today."

"And you have to 'Skip to My Lou' as a solo in gym," said Michael. "Fly's in the buttermilk, shoo, fly, shoo," he sang. "Why would anybody want to write a song about bugs in milk?"

"Class," Mr. Marconi said, "as you read today about the Cascade Mountains and the perils the pioneers faced, I want you to be thinking about what you'll do when the time comes to cross them. There's a small fort and trading post at the Walla Walla River, before you reach the mountains. You can stop there to wait out the winter. Or you can try to forge ahead to claim some Oregon land."

"But you might die in a mountain pass.

Everybody knows that," Zach said. "If you throw the die and it comes up six, you don't make it. My sister did that last year."

"That's true. And some of you, sadly, will have more passes to cross than others. Some of you have been losing points by not updating your journals, by not completing your math, or by not cooperating with each other on the trail. Each year at least one group hasn't survived the mountains."

"But..."

"I just want you to be thinking about it. You won't make your final decision until Thursday."

"That's easy," Marilou told Michael. "We wait."

"No way," said Michael. "We cross."

"People, that's a choice for another day. Right now we're going to do some one-room schoolhouse work. Get out your slates and chalk for a short spelling test. Ready? Your first word is *stampede.* Even a small barking dog could cause a stampede. Stampede."

By nine-thirty Wagon Train Seven was doing math, figuring out how many calories they'd use to chop their wood and load their wagons and how much food they'd need to make up for it. Dr. Martin Jones was working it out alone. His wife was not there.

At ten-ten they were stitching up pieces of a cradle quilt in art class when the door opened. It was Dinah. She struck a pose in the doorway, her arms open wide, so they could all get their eyes full. Then she loped in.

Everyone laughed.

She stuck out her front teeth, wiggled her nose like a rabbit with hay fever, then headed for the chair next to Orin.

"My trusty husband will show me how," she told the art teacher. "Well, dear?" she asked Orin.

"You got the teeth right, but you forgot to cross your eyes," he whispered. "The nose part was new, though. Nice touch."

"Look, I didn't want Lydia to make a stupid face, but the kids were all laughing, so I had to."

He stared at her and shook his head. "How could they *not* laugh? You made them. I hate to tell you, Mrs. Jones, but you look...strange. That thing on your head. It's weird. What are you thinking?"

"I'm thinking I never knew you were such a big fashion guy."

She pulled a needle from the pincushion in front of her. Looking over the scraps of old fabric that kids had brought from home, she finally chose a small flowered square.

A graph of the quilt design they'd made on computer lay in the middle of the table. Marilou leaned over it. "Where's that cute green scarf with the yellow dots, Mrs. J.? Amazing hat, by the way. Where'd you get it?"

Orin watched Dinah try to thread her needle. "You must be a fantastic gardener," he said. "Not only do you have a green thumb, you've got green fingers."

She shrugged and tried to tie a knot in the thread. Her fingers weren't nearly as green as they had been.

"You need a thimble?" Michael asked, handing her one from the sewing basket.

No one said anything about her weird blue-green hair. No one said anything because no one could see it. The hat she was wearing, tied very tightly under her chin in a big bow, was a cotton print bonnet with a wide, floppy brim. Every strand of her hair was stuffed inside.

"This is a genuine pioneer-type sunbonnet," Dinah explained, still looking down. "My grandmother made it." In fact, that's why she was late. Her grandmother had sewn the whole hat by hand that very morning.

All weekend long, Dinah had *not* shampooed her hair. Several times, when Nanna had told her to, she had stood in the shower and got it wet. But she hadn't really washed it, and the color had stayed strong.

When the Monday morning damping-down still hadn't dimmed the green, Dinah had said, "Too bad," and curled up in a soft chair with the TV on.

Nanna had turned it off. "Oh, no you don't. I didn't say you weren't going to school. I said you weren't going to school looking like *that*."

"But *that's* what I look like." Dinah crossed her arms.

"I was certain that color would fade," Nanna said. "I'll think of something. But I won't be responsible for your playing hookey. When I was little, that was frowned upon."

"My grandmother remembers the olden days," Dinah told Sarah and Orin.

"She may have made a genuine hat, but she made it way too big," Orin said.

"It's got to be big to keep the sun off my nose. It's a *sun* bonnet."

"But there are Hot Wheels cars all over it. I doubt they had Hot Wheels in 1846. I could be wrong, of course."

Nanna had cut the bonnet out of the only fabric she could find—Boris's pillow case. It had, she said, just the right amount of cloth. When Boris saw the Hot Wheels hat he shrieked. When Dinah saw it she said, "No way."

"It's the only way I can think of," said Nanna. "If you take this off at school and they send you home because of inappropriate hair," she had warned Dinah, "I will be upset. I want you to know that."

"You don't have to wear that sunbonnet thing just because your grandmother made it," Sarah told her. "I mean, it was probably very nice of her to try to help you look like a pioneer, but you could take it off now and she'd never know."

"I think it's cute. I really, really do," Marilou said. "You think she'd make me one? Can I try it on later?"

"Later," Dinah said. Much later, she thought.

"Hey, Dino," Clyde called.

"My name is Lydia," she told him. "And don't you forget it."

"You late because you're scared?" he asked her.

"Shaking in her high-top boots." Orin shook his head. "Tell me, does the big bad wolf scare you, Goldilocks?"

Dinah pulled her bonnet down even closer over her hair. "Why did you call me Goldilocks?"

"I don't know. Clyde was just baring his baby-fangs."

"Well, I'm not Goldilocks. And I'm not scared."

"Vroooom, vroooom," said Clyde. "Funny hat. Not funny enough to save you, but funny." He pointed and laughed. A few kids laughed with him.

And he kept pointing and laughing all through Journal Writing, through some of Science, and a through a little bit of lunch. But by the time they got to Meg's room to travel across the prairie, the joke had worn thin. Nobody cared that Lydia Jones was wearing a Hot Wheels bonnet.

In Meg's room the shades were

drawn and the lights were out.

"Settle down in your circle," Meg said. "You've got a long way to go." She looked serious. "Your leader has quit. You've given up most of your horses in payment for one rash act. Some of you tend to argue instead of discuss. You've already lost twenty-seven points. I suppose you know this wagon train is in big trouble."

12

☞All in Favor Say Aye

Clyde stood up. "Hey, listen up! I, Ernest the Pioneer, have got something to say."

"Sorry, Ernest," Meg told him, "but it'll have to wait till morning." The wagon train was in its circle, but the lights were still off. She waited two beats.

"The lookout has fired his rifle to wake you up," she began. "It's four A.M., mid-July, and even this early, the air is scorching hot. You should have reached Independence Rock by the Fourth of July. But see your pin on the wall map? You haven't even crossed the North Platte

126

River." She clicked on half of the room's lights. "Okay, travelers, rise and shine."

Sarah stood up, yawned and stretched. "I say let's do all the chores and then elect our leader."

"Good thinking," Orin told her.

"'Good thinking,' like he's the teacher or something," Clyde said to Jessica. She rolled her eyes.

"What did you want to say so bad?" Marilou asked Clyde.

"Later," he told her. "You're gonna love it."

Dinah gathered up an imaginary bundle of sticks and laid them on the low-smoldering imaginary fire. "Fuel's low," she told them. "It's hard to find when there aren't trees."

"I'll get some men to herd in the livestock," Zach said, and he left the circle.

"I'll get some of the older kids to help me take down the tents and load the wagons," Michael announced, and pretended to do it.

"I've got to cook again, don't I?" Marilou

asked. "Okay, but I'm really, really tired of johnnycakes. Besides, the cornmeal got all wet last time we crossed a river. And the eggs we buried in the cornmeal are either all used up or rotten. So I'm grilling buffalo steaks for breakfast. And you know what I'm putting on them? I'll tell you what. You'd never guess. Gunpowder."

Jessica looked up. "Clyde, she's going to poison us."

"Am not. They did that when they ran out of salt and pepper. A dash of gunpowder for flavor. No joke. I, personally, read it in this pioneer cookbook."

"That's sick," Clyde said.

"Something else, too," Marilou went on. "Our bread has *worms* in it. You've got to shake it"—she flicked her wrist—"to get them out."

"Maybe we should just eat the worms," Sarah said. "At least they wouldn't be tough, like that jerky stuff. I'll make some coffee with the yucky green water."

"Be sure you boil it," Orin warned.

"That water's crawling with mosquito larvae and germs."

"Dr. Jones," Meg broke in, "you don't know about germs in the 1840's. But something has made Ernest and Jane sick. They seem to have woken with fevers and chills. See what you can do to help them out."

Orin grinned and strolled over to Clyde and Jessica. "Hi, folks. Might be dysentery you've contracted," he told them, leaning over and feeling their foreheads. "Lot of that going round. Had any chills, nausea, trots? Tell you what. I'll just make a deep cut in each of your arms to drain off some of that tainted blood. One cup each ought to make you feel better fast."

"You're not gonna slash me." Clyde moved back.

"Me either," said Jessica.

Orin held up an imaginary knife. "Ernest and Jane," he said solemnly, "I saw a comet in the sky last night and that often causes dysentery. It's a known fact. We've got to get rid of that bad blood fast, so good healthy blood can take its place. Now, I don't have any blood-sucking leeches with me, so I've got to use my scalpel."

"Wait, just wait. You're gonna *get* it," Clyde said.

"Your little girl's fine, though. I won't bleed her."

"I object," Jessica said loudly. "Like Clyde's father says, we could be doing long division or making other good use of our time."

"Blood letting is accepted medical practice," Orin told her. "Or I could try blistering. That sometimes helps. But long division never helped a fever. Give me your arm."

"You make me so mad," Clyde said. "Get lost. We'll drink our Super Elixir. I bought three bottles of it."

Orin shrugged. "I wouldn't if I were you. That stuff'll do you more harm than good. It's mostly alcohol. Certainly don't give it to your daughter. It's like drinking gin."

Meg turned all the lights on. "The sun

has come up," she said, "and the storm clouds have blown to the east."

She had been whispering instructions to Zach, who stepped forward into the middle of the imaginary bonfire.

Dinah scooted him out and threw on another bundle of twigs.

"Okay, you guys," Zach said. "Our leader quit. Now we've got to elect a new one. Any ideas?"

Michael put his hands over his head as though the sky might be falling. "I'm sorry," he told them.

"Well, my husband is a good person," Sarah said. "I nominate you."

Zach shook his head. "Forget it. When Michael—Hiram—made a mistake, everybody was really down on him. No, thanks. I've got this plan, though. What if we don't go on at all? What's so wrong with that? What if we just decide to camp right here and not go to Oregon? Meg, is that okay?"

"It's your option," Meg told him. "This is your story."

"We *can't* stay here," Sarah said. "Either

it's other people's land or it's no good for farming. And there aren't any trees. Besides, if we stayed it would cost us money and we don't have much left. Land's free in Oregon. All we've got to do is claim it. That's what Mr. Bilkum said."

"You're absolutely right," Orin told Sarah. "You have a clear head. *You* should be our fearless leader."

Sarah smiled. "You're right. But Clara's got five kids under ten years old and one of them just got bit by a rattlesnake, remember, doctor?"

"I do. I sucked out the venom myself."

"Big deal," Clyde said. "Big fat deal."

"Maybe Ernest or Jane would like to be leader," Sarah suggested.

"Well, I just might," Clyde began.

"That whole family's under the weather with dysentery," Orin told them.

Clyde narrowed his eyes at Orin and crossed his arms.

Dinah took a deep breath. "I've been thinking. You know how we voted against Marilou—Mrs. Winchester—before? Well, she's been working hard. And she's been reading a lot, and she cares about what's going on, so maybe she..."

"Me?" Marilou asked. "You want me?"

"Maybe," Dinah said. "I just thought..."

"Well, okay. But you know what? For starters, I'd make us go back home. So anybody who wants to turn the train around can vote for me."

"All in favor?" Zach said. Nobody was.

"How about Lydia?" Dinah asked. She pulled her bonnet tighter. "I'm tall, so at least everybody would know where I stand."

Michael laughed. "That's true," he said.

"I'm strong," Dinah went on. "I was a sales clerk in Pennsylvania, so I know how to deal with people."

"You do not," said Clyde. "You or Orin either. Besides, I've got a complaint against you and now's the time to tell it." He stood up, crossed his arms, and began. "This morning at round-up I noticed that my mules and pigs and my horse were all gone. Disappeared. Nowhere in sight. And the last ones I saw near them were Dinah and Orin."

"Lydia and Marty," Orin corrected him.

"I say they stole my animals. And we've got rules. Marilou wrote them down. One of them is that rustlers get thrown out of the train. Without bread and water." He smiled. "So I vote we kick out the Dino and the Shrimp."

"Stay in character," Meg warned him.

"I *am* in character."

"Well, we didn't do it," said Orin. "So much for threats."

"It's your word against mine. And I've got witnesses. I bet you don't. First off, my wife saw them do it."

"I did," said Jessica. "Maybe...will this cut our grade?"

"And Hepsibah saw them, too. Remember?"

Marilou bit her lip. "You want me to say the Joneses stole your mules and pigs?"

"And our only horse. Come on, Marilou," Clyde whispered. "They'll have to sit out the rest of the week and just watch us. Meg says it's our story. We can do it if we want to. What are rules for?" He raised his voice. "And Clara and Hiram, you saw them. Just say you did."

Nobody said anything. Michael got up from the circle and walked away.

"Wait a minute. If we stole your mules, pigs, and fine riding horse," Dinah asked, "where are they? We're out here in the middle of nowhere. There's no place to hide them." She shook her head. "Ernest, you've shot yourself in the foot."

"Lydia's right. You made that up," said Marilou. "I bet we've got a rule against lying."

Michael came back to the circle. "You'll be glad to know that I just checked the animals," he said. "All of them are there."

"You're kidding. Come on. Mine too?" Clyde asked.

"Especially yours," Michael said.

"Really? So who gets punished now?" Sarah asked. "What do you say? Forty lashes?"

"You didn't mean it, anyway, Clyde, did

you?" Jessica asked him. "Weren't you kidding?"

"Sure. It was a joke. Can't you take a joke?" Clyde laughed, too loud.

"Very funny," Dinah told him.

"Big waste of time," said Sarah. "Let's vote."

"All in favor of Lydia for leader?" Zach asked.

Clara, Hiram, and Dr. Jones voted "Aye."

"Opposed?"

Marilou said, "I'm not sure. Not everybody really likes her. I think I say no."

"You got that right," Clyde sat down. "I vote no."

"Me, too," Jessica agreed. "She can't take a joke."

Zach looked at Meg to see what he should do. She didn't look back. It was seven minutes to bell time.

"Okay, I vote no, too," Zach said. "We've got a wagon train here, not a clown parade."

"You'd be voting for Lydia Jones,"

Dinah told him, "not me. She's different. She's not a clown."

"Four to three," said Clyde. "Lydia loses."

"Can I vote for myself?" Dinah asked.

Jessica shook her head.

"Sure she can," Sarah told them. "You see presidents do it all the time on TV. I mean, you would have if they'd had TV, which, of course, they didn't."

"I don't know. I guess if presidents can," Zach said, "but it's getting late."

"Then I do," Dinah said. "I vote for Lydia, for me."

Zach sighed. "Okay, great, so the bell's about to ring and it's tied. What do we do now? Anybody want to change their vote?"

"We're losing points," said Jessica. "I can feel them dripping away by the gazillions."

"Maybe we should start over," Zach suggested.

Orin shook his head. "It's too late."

"All right," Marilou told them, "I'm not sure this is the right thing, but I'm going to say yes. Sometimes she's got good ideas. Like, she nominated me. So, aye. I vote aye for Lydia."

"Five to three," Orin announced. "Strike up the band."

"No confetti. Hold down the cheering," Dinah told them, but nobody laughed. "Okay, we're all packed, let's go." And they stood up and started to walk slowly in a big circle, even Jessica and Clyde.

"Freeze," Meg called, flicking the switch. They all stopped. She left the lights off.

"It's early evening. There's been a steady, light rain all day, the tail of the storm. It's left the ground sodden. You're approaching the North Platte River and have to decide whether to cross tonight or wait until tomorrow. Remember, you're running way behind schedule and snow comes early in the mountains. You've got to weigh that."

"Trying to cross the river at night, though, that would be a major mistake," Michael said. "Wagon Train Two did it. I know, I was talking to them, and they lost lots of cows."

"Right," Dinah agreed. "It's bad enough in daytime. I say we camp on the banks. All in favor?"

There was a general "Aye." Everyone but Clyde and Jessica.

"No?" Lydia asked them. "You think we should try to cross over?"

"Whatever you say," Clyde told her. "I say we move on, but if you say we don't, we don't."

"But it's a river and I can't swim," Jessica said, getting into it. "And it's dark."

Orin whispered in Dinah's ear.

"Oh, I forgot. Listen, I completely forgot. Does it have to be today?" she asked him.

He just looked at her.

"I guess it does. Fellow wagon trainers, there's a small problem," she announced, "we *can't* cross the river tonight."

"Can't?" asked Jessica. "Why not?" Like now she really wanted to.

"Just can't. The thing is," Dinah told them, "I, Lydia Jones, am not feeling so good."

"She feels poorly," Orin said. "You better lie down."

Dinah sat on the floor.

"Breathe deeply," Orin told her.

"I've got a great idea," said Clyde. "Slash her arms. Drain off a bucket of blood and she'll be fine."

"She's dying. Untie her bonnet." Marilou pulled at the bow under Dinah's chin and it flapped free.

"No she's not," said Orin.

Dinah grabbed the hat. "No I'm not. It's just that it's July. And on the sheet we got, it says that in July I've got to have a baby."

"A baby? You *can't* have a baby," Zach told her. "We just made you leader."

"Give her room," Sarah said.

"Push," Orin told her.

"What's that supposed to mean?" Dinah asked.

"They always say it on TV."

"I think," Meg told them, "we can just assume the baby has been born and it's a fine, healthy..."

140

"Girl," said Dinah. "Anybody have a blanket?"

It was one minute to bell time.

"Dinah!" Orin gasped. "This is awful. Something terrible has happened. You are genuinely sick. It's your hair. Your hair's turned green."

Everyone stopped and stared.

With the bow untied, Dinah's sunbonnet had worked itself loose and fallen to her shoulders. She put her hand to her head. "It's okay," she said.

"The hat did it," Marilou explained. "The color bled right out of the Hot Wheels into your hair."

They all moved closer.

"She's got pea-green hair." Jessica touched it.

"Dinahsaurus green," Clyde said.

"Having babies on the trail will do that to you," Dinah told them.

The bell rang.

"Hail to the green chief," said Orin. "All hail."

13

☞And Then the Mosquito Ate...

"**I** never personally thought you would ever in a million years dye your hair green," Marilou said. "Was Mr. Marconi mad yesterday? Can I sit here?" Marilou made a place for herself between Kaat and Dinah.

Kaat's Wagon Train Six and Dinah's Seven were sitting together in a big circle on the floor of Mr. Marconi's room. They were together for storytelling.

"I mean, that was really, really something," Marilou went on. "I told Brandi and Tiffani and they couldn't believe it, either."

"He wasn't mad exactly," Dinah told her. "He just said to wash it out."

"Did you say it was my fault?" Kaat asked. "You could have."

"Of course not."

Dinah was wearing her sunbonnet to school again. This time, though, it wasn't on her head. It hung loose like a knapsack down her blue-checked blouse. And she wore a long brown skirt of her grandmother's, its hem wet from the snow.

"I told him it was a big mistake."

"Oh, yes, I think it was a really, really big mistake," Marilou said. "It's not a bit *you.* Tiffani could get away with it, but you're not the green-hair type at all."

"So, Lydia," Zach called. "Does that new baby of yours have green hair, too? If he does, he's going to knock 'em dead out west."

"She," Dinah told him, "has green eyes. And her name is Mildred Erika."

"People," said Mr. Marconi, stepping into the middle of the circle, "we're about to begin. Be sure you're sitting with the rest of your train."

"Family calls," Kaat said and moved next to Charles.

"It's August on the trail today," Mr. Marconi went on. "You've been gone since March and most of you are exhausted. You're hungry for the food you grew up with and you're lonely for the people you left behind. You are beginning to doubt your future."

Sarah leaned across Marilou. "What Clyde tried to do to you and Orin was not nice," she whispered to Dinah. "Boys! And by the way, you didn't get all the green out."

"No," Marilou agreed, "but it's a different green."

Dinah had washed her hair twice and rinsed it with cider vinegar, just like her grandmother said to. When that didn't work, Kaat had called Barbara's Beauty Shop for help.

"All right, pioneers," Mr. Marconi went on, "for the rest of the week you'll be telling some of the tall tales you've written. We don't have time for them on the trail with Meg, so we'll just have to pretend we've got our campfire here. I know you have some fine stories to share. Who's first?"

"So, what'd you do to it?" Marilou whispered to Dinah. "Yesterday it was like..."

"Pond scum," Dinah said.

"Right. Right. Today it's more like...lime."

"Lemon," Dinah told her. "Kaat squeezed four lemons on my head, pulp and all. So I'm part Kool-Aid and part lemonade. I'm a walking fruit-juice stand."

Marilou laughed. "My mom would have been mad."

"My mom's out of town."

"Lucky."

"Hepsibah Winchester," said Mr. Marconi, "I take it you are volunteering to be our first storyteller."

"Sure," Marilou said, and she stood up, flipped her hair, and began. Her story was about "this really, really tall girl named Paulette Wart" who had "this really, really smart ox named Brave." What Paulette did was pick a big bunch of "humongous redwood trees." Then she got on Brave's back and they rode "really really high" until they landed on the moon. From there Paulette whirled the trees round and round in the air and brushed the dust from outer space off of all the stars. And that, Marilou said, was when the stars began to shine.

"That was really, really good," Orin told Marilou when she sat down.

"Yes," said Marilou.

"Paulette was tall," Dinah mentioned.

"She couldn't have done it if she wasn't," said Marilou.

Charles, leader of Wagon Train Six, was next. He read eight pages about a yellow dragon who lived in a deep cave in the old West. It spit up sulphur-water geysers that smelled like wet sneakers. This dragon, whose name was Yellowstone, chased away a whole wagon train of polluting pioneers and the forest animals lived happily ever after.

All the kids in Wagon Train Six clapped and shouted, especially Kaat.

Then Zach stood up. Zach could draw, so his story had almost as many pictures as words. He showed and told about a bunch of wooly mammoths. They had a contest spitting pickle slices across the Grand Canyon.

"As tales go, these are very tall," said Mr. Marconi. "We have time, I think, for one more."

Michael held up his hand.

"Hiram Winchester," he called on Michael.

"This isn't very good, but..."

"He read it to me. It's gross," Zach said.

"...here goes," Michael went on. "It's called 'The Mosquito.'" He took a deep breath and began. "The worst thing about our trip out west wasn't the dust storm of black pepper. It wasn't the mud that was like a river of molasses. It wasn't even the hairy tarantulas we had to eat raw. The worst thing was the mosquitoes."

"It's getting grosser," Zach told them.

"The mosquitoes were big," Michael read on.

"How big?" Orin asked, and Michael grinned.

"They were so big that when our last ox tripped and broke his legs, we caught one of the *baby* giant mosquitoes and put a harness on it. Then we flicked our whip and that baby giant mosquito pulled all four of our wagons right through the molasses river and up over the Cascade Mountains. No problem.

"But when we landed, the mosquito was hungry and that *was* a problem, because when those babies bite you, you stay bit. They suck out all your blood except for maybe one drop.

"We knew this because once that same mosquito had bit this guy in our wagon train who was caught lying. His name was..."

"Ernest," said Orin.

"How you'd guess?" Michael asked him.

"No fair," Clyde called.

But Michael went on. "In one bite the mosquito had sucked out Ernest's blood so that all that was left was one big, fat, humongous itch. We had to roll him along the trail so the tumbleweed could scratch it.

"So we knew we had to feed that mosquito fast. Those prairie mosquitoes weren't just blood suckers, either. They were meat eaters, too."

"This is the grossest part," Zach said.

"So to keep it from biting us, we took the dead ox that had broken its legs and we cooked it over the campfire. The mosquito smelled the char-grilled ox. It flew to the fire. It stuck out its tongue and it licked.

"'Blechhhh,' the mosquito said. This was a talking mosquito. And it flew *away* from the ox. 'Blechhhh,' it said again. It looked around at all of us and it licked its lips. First it headed toward Doctor Jones, but he was too small."

"All *right*," Orin said.

"And then it flew right up to Lydia Jones, but when it opened its mouth, the giant baby mosquito decided that she was..."

"Too *big*," Dinah called. "Saved by my size."

"...*much* too big," Michael went on, smiling. "And then it saw poor itchy Ernest's wife, Jane, and decided that she was..."

And they all—all but Clyde and Jessica—yelled, "Just right!"

Jessica held up her hand. "No fair," she said.

"But," Michael went on, "Hepsibah Winchester, the cook, had an idea. I bet that meat needs salt, she thought, and she ran to get it, but she saw that the salt and pepper had both been washed away in the vast molasses river.

"The mosquito landed on poor Jane's shoulder and was just about to take a big bite of..."

"Stop it," said Jessica.

"Hiram," Mr. Marconi warned.

"It's just a tall tale," Michael told him. "So, this big bug was starting to stab Jane's neck when Hepsibah remembered something she'd read in a cookbook. If you don't have salt, it had said, you can use..."

"*Gunpowder,*" Marilou shouted. "It really said that."

"And Hepsibah took out a horn of gunpowder that had stayed dry, and she sprinkled it all over the char-grilled ox. Well, that mosquito let go of Jane, who tasted a little sour anyway."

"I do not," said Jessica.

"And the mosquito smacked its lips and lit into that ox and he ate it all up in one gulp. He liked it so much that he flew over the campfire looking for more, and he got so close to the flames that..."

The room was so quiet you could hear a mosquito buzz.

"He got so close that... *KA-POWEEE!* the mosquito exploded. And the blood and the bug bones broke into so many billions of bits that they flew way up in the sky and they became a new galaxy known as...the Mosquito Way."

Kids started to clap, but Michael went on.

"But then, we didn't have anything to pull our wagons. That was okay, though, because the mosquito had already flown us across the Cascade Mountains and we

151

were safe at last and we all, even Ernest, lived happily ever after."

"Michael and I both wrote about stars," Marilou whispered to Dinah. "Did you notice that? I think he likes me."

All the kids clapped. All except Clyde and Jessica.

"An excellent tale," said Orin.

"You know what I liked best?" Dinah asked him. "It wasn't about a dinosaur and it wasn't about a shrimp."

14

☞**Not So Dear Diary**

August 15, 1846

Dear Diary,

August is not the best of months. Mildred Erika cries a lot and Buster is not a good baby-sitter. While he's very bright and short, he is, after all, only eight. He refuses to change her diapers. Which is understandable. They aren't disposables. There hasn't been much rain and babies are hard to clean up when you don't have water. All we can do is scrape the excrement off and air out the diapers until they're dry. That's all we can do, over and over again, until we find water to wash them in. After a while you get used to the smell.

Ernest and Jane still disapprove of Lydia as wagon train leader. She's a good one, though. A passing guide tried to sell us a map to a fast "cutoff." But while some wanted to try it, Lydia said no. We later found out from another wagon train that it wasn't fast at all, but led to the desert.

The rest of us get along well now. We all worked together at the North Platte River. We had to. There seemed to be more mud than water so that our wagons were sinking in up to their axles. No wheels came off, though. Our blacksmith, Johann, has been working on them nights.

Lydia said I had to leave the pump organ behind. She said the wagon would be so heavy that the mud would suck us in if I didn't. There wasn't time to play a march on it or even a minuet. We're way behind schedule. I hope someone will save it before the rains come. Maybe someone else will bring it to Oregon. I really love that pump organ.

A good thing happened to Lydia. Clara showed up today wearing a sunbonnet. Clara's is yellow with little blue flowers on it. When she saw Clara's, Lydia took her bonnet off her shoulders and tied it on her head again. Of course, then you couldn't see her interesting hair, which is unique on the prairie.

No one, I think, is quite like Lydia.

September is the key month. We voted to cross the mountains. All the other wagon trains that we know of decided the same. It's hard to come this far and then wait. But that means we will have to travel through dangerous mountain passes. Will we make it? Pray God we will.

Martin Jones (called Big Marty by friends)

August 15, 1846
Dear Mother,
We are well. Mostly. Except for that time our little Sophie got bit by a rattler. And when Johann Junior fell out of the wagon

155

twice. The wheels missed him both times. He's a lucky kid. I bet he'll live to be a hundred.

You were right. This is a lot of work. I didn't know it would be so bad when I said I'd make the trip. The worst part is that everybody doesn't get along. You're always thinking there's going to be a fight.

It's only been a few months, but I bet you and Pa wouldn't know me if I knocked on your door, which I wish I could. The sun has made me very tan, even though I've started wearing the sunbonnet you made for me. And the blue dress I wear every day doesn't have a white collar and cuffs like it used to. They're brown. The dust of Kansas did it. And the hem of the skirt is black with Platte River mud. I bet you wouldn't invite me in to tea.

At night we tell tall tales by the fire. Tomorrow is my turn. I'm going to do the one you used to tell us about the Fuzzy Dust Bunny that scares away shadow monsters who live under the bed. The children will love it and it makes me think of real beds. It also makes me think of when home wasn't in a wagon.

Very soon we're going over the mountains. It's bad in the mountains. We've heard a lot of stories about avalanches and sudden storms. I don't let the children know, but I'm scared. I think we all are.

Two trail guides have stopped with us on their way back east. They'll post this letter to you. I will write again from Oregon.

Love,
Clara

August 15, 1846
Not so dear Diary,

This whole thing is a big mess and it's not our fault. Not mine, anyway. They both think they're so smart, especially Dr. Shrimp. And the big one acts like she really is *The Big One*. Her hair is green and nobody will tell me why. I think it's a disease. I think the heat fried her brain.

They won the big vote. Three of us—me

and my wife and Hepsibah Winchester—all voted yes to camping out over the winter near Fort Walla Walla. I told them why we should do it. We were too tired. We didn't have enough food. Hepsibah did, too, but they wouldn't listen. It was their five to our three. So that means we have to cross the Cascade Mountains next month. For sure there'll be blizzards and we'll die up there. It's because of them we've got three passes to cross. That's three big throws of the die. We could get caught in any of them.

We should stay in the valley. What's the big hurry, I say.

Anyway, I've carved my name on some rocks along the way so people will know I was here. That's one good thing about this trip, the big rocks. One of them looked like a cathedral, everyone said. I never saw one, so I wouldn't know. I went to see all the rocks, though. And you can find Ernest Ames written on Chimney Rock, Scott's Bluff, Register Cliff, and lots of others. If my brother from Richmond follows me out here, he'll see it. And if things keep going the way they are now, that's all that'll be left of me.

I should have stayed home.

They'll be sorry.

Your writer,

Ernest

15

"Did we lose points because of her green hair?" Clyde asked. "Because if we did..."

Meg shook her head.

"This is so unfair," Marilou complained. "I mean it. We worked really, really hard on this trip. I, personally, did. And now all we've got to do is throw a six on a dumb die and we'll die dead. I ask you, is that fair?"

"No," Meg said. "It's not. You're absolutely right. I've gone through this six times today and I don't like it any more than you do. I hate it. I keep telling Mr.

Marconi that it's mean, but he says they've always done it this way."

She sat down with them in the circle. "I hate this so much. Mr. Marconi says it teaches you that natural disasters can strike at any time, but you're practically babies, for heaven's sake."

"We are not," Dinah said. "We're eleven, most of us."

Meg lowered her voice. "Listen, I tell you what. If you want to skip this part and just *say* you made it over the mountains, I'll go along with it."

They all stared at her.

"Well, I don't know. I don't want to die," said Marilou, "but wouldn't that be, like, cheating?"

"You'd let us?" Michael asked her.

"All the other teams threw the die, didn't they?" Dinah asked.

"All the others did," said Meg. "But none of them had to do it more than twice. You've lost sixty-three points altogether. And it's one throw for each twenty points."

"Three throws," said Sarah.

"I'm sorry you have so many," Meg told them. "I genuinely am. Maybe I was too..."

"It's not *your* fault," Orin said.

"I don't know," she went on. "Maybe that gunshot didn't have to hit..."

"Did anybody lose yet?" Clyde asked.

"I'm scared," said Jessica.

Meg bit her lip. "Forget it. Let's just get started."

"What happened?" Marilou asked. "What team died? Tell us."

"You won't let us lose, will you?" Jessica asked her.

"If we're going to do this, let's just do it," Meg said. "Just forget it. It's time to travel. Tuck your children in the wagons and lead those tired oxen of yours up the mountain trail."

They all stood up. Dinah and Sarah both had on their bonnets. Marilou had brought a plaid shawl from home, which she wrapped tight around her shoulders. Orin was wearing a black cowboy hat that made him six inches taller.

"The clouds are low and the wind is

sharp," Meg said. "There might be a storm or there might not. Weather is all a matter of chance."

She flicked the lights off for the last time.

The shades were drawn, but outside, snowflakes were falling like feathers, big and light.

Wagon Train Seven began to trudge in a circle, slowly.

"You're coming up to the first pass," Meg told them. "Time to stop."

From a brown paper bag she pulled out a three-inch die, white and fuzzy with black dots. It looked used, as if it had been hanging for years from someone's car mirror.

"Who has to throw it?" Zach asked, eyeing the big white cube in Meg's hand.

"The green-haired dragon," Clyde said.

"Lydia," Jessica told him. "Her name is Lydia."

"Do I have to?" Dinah asked. No one else volunteered.

"I can't. I'm holding the baby," Orin said.

"Before you throw it, you're supposed to kiss it. Let me," Marilou said. "Close your eyes and wish." She kissed her fingers and put them on the die.

"Close your eyes and wish," Jessica repeated.

Dinah closed her eyes, shook the die between her hands, threw it up high in the air, and wished for a two. She didn't look when it landed.

"One," Marilou shouted. "It landed on one."

They all clapped and shouted.

"The sky is *blue*," Zach said.

Meg smiled. "Well, onward. Time to go. Once more over the mountain."

Wagon Train Seven began to walk faster. One down, two to go. Jessica was skipping.

"They'll be comin' round the mountain when they come," Dinah sang.

"They'll be comin' round the mountain when they come," the pioneers sang with her.

The whole group was running by the time they'd finished two verses. "They'll be driving six white horses, they'll be driving six white horses, they'll be driving six white horses when they come."

"Freeze," Meg said. "This is pass number two. It's steep here, and very nearly impassable. But I know you can do it."

"Who throws this time?" Dinah asked.

"You again," Clyde said.

"You," said Jessica. "Close your eyes and wish."

Marilou kissed the fuzzy cube. Dinah threw it in the air. This time she watched.

It landed with four dots up.

"This is fun," Sarah said. "I knew we could do it."

"It's a piece of cake," Michael told them. "Hurry up and throw it again while we're winning."

"Okay," Meg agreed, "go ahead."

Marilou gave the die one last kiss. Dinah threw it up so high it touched the ceiling and when it fell to the floor it rolled and rolled and rolled before it finally stopped. On six.

"Six," Jessica said. "That's a six."

"Wait a minute." Marilou picked it up. "I kissed it. I wished. It's no fair. Let's throw it again."

"You made your choice," said Meg. "You can't go back on it now. The snow is falling so hard you can't see the path. You can't see each other." She turned away from them. "Ahead you hear what sounds like thunder, but it isn't thunder. It's a rush of snow, an avalanche pounding down the mountain. There is no way you can go forward."

Marilou pulled her shawl tighter. They all moved closer together.

"Then we'll go back," Orin said.

"A boulder breaks off a cliff behind you," Meg went on.

"You said we could skip it altogether. Why can't we throw the die one more time?" Jessica asked.

"I didn't want to go in the first place," Marilou said. "We only went because we were losers."

"I am not a loser," Michael told her. "We

just didn't have enough farm land. We *had* to go west. We had to. You know that. They told us we'd get rich. Everybody said so.

"I lost us points by shooting," Michael went on. "But I didn't mean to hurt him. I thought that's what people *did*. I thought you had to shoot to win. I had this gun..."

"It wasn't you," Clyde told him. "After you, we got the worst leader in the world who made us go over the mountains."

Orin shook his head. "We voted."

"I voted no," Clyde said. "I wanted to stay in Walla Walla."

"Me, too," said Jessica.

Marilou sat down. "And me."

"Majority ruled," said Orin.

"But we were *right*," Marilou told him. "See. That's the thing. You were wrong. And now we're all going to die." She turned away from them and started to cry.

Meg switched on the light. "Please don't," she said. "It's all right."

"Marilou, I'm sorry." Michael reached out and patted her arm. "I really am."

She brushed his hand off her arm as if

it were a locust from the August plague. "And don't call me Marilou. I'm Hepsibah and I've got a right to be mad. I don't want to die and I've got two really nice girls and I don't want them to die either." She sat down and crossed her arms.

"My kids didn't even want to come," said Sarah. "They're so little. And there are five of them. Five."

"Maybe we shouldn't give up. We could try to get out," Michael told them. "You guys, turn the oxen around. Turn the wagon around. We'll go back the way we came."

"You can't do it," Meg told them. "The mountain ledge you're on is too narrow. Sometimes they were caught."

"We can *try* harder than they did," Sarah said.

"They tried very hard." Meg explained. "It was real life for them."

Clyde yawned. "Big deal. Big fat deal. It's not real for us."

"*Do* something," Jessica told him.

"Use a whip on the oxen," Sarah said.

"A whip won't move an ox with a broken leg," Meg told her.

"*We* don't have broken legs. And we're really strong. We can walk." Dinah started back. "I'll go for help."

"No, you can't," said Meg. "All you've eaten is tough, dry buffalo jerky and wormy bread, and you're *not* strong."

"Okay, we'll slide down the mountain. Like skiers. We can do it. We can slide back down the mountain."

"My girls can't," said Marilou. "They're too little."

"And neither can we." Michael sighed. "It's not like a ski slope."

"The trip is over," Meg announced, and she flicked the lights off and on and off and then on again.

"No fair," said Jessica, and then it was quiet.

"I'm sorry this group lost," Meg said. "You made mistakes, but so did everybody. For the most part you did well. Truly."

Dinah rubbed her eyes. "I think we went to heaven," she said.

"Can we go home now?" Marilou asked. She took out a tissue and blew her nose. "Since we're all dead, anyway."

"You're due in Mr. Marconi's room in five minutes," Meg told them. "You have to finish your journals and then get ready for tomorrow's party."

"How can we finish our journals if we're dead?" Orin asked. "I just wondered."

"Do we go as ghosts?" Clyde asked. "Whoooooooooo." He waved his fingers in the air and started to run around the room.

"Stop it," said Jessica.

"Enough, Ernest," Meg said. "I'm sorry I only know your pioneer names. Anyway, now that you've thrown a six, your characters change. I don't know what you'll call yourselves, but you're Oregon settlers who welcome those pioneers who made it safely. Five of this year's wagon trains arrived in Oregon. Two did not."

"Who all lost?" Sarah asked.

"Your group and train number five. They lost on the first throw."

"You're kidding," Marilou said. "Wagon Train Five? That means Brandi and Tiffani died, too!" She shook off her shawl and stood up. "This is wonderful. This is really excellent. Now all three of us are angels."

Party On West

The boom box was booming out folk music. Frontier folk never heard it so loud. "Skip to My Lou" bounced off the walls and ceiling and echoed into all the corners of the multipurpose room.

The purpose of the multipurpose room this Friday morning was the Welcome to Oregon party. The wagon trains had gathered at nine-fifteen to eat, do-si-do, and then leave the place clean before eleven. That's when lunch was the purpose of the multipurpose room. Gym, usually the purpose at nine-fifteen, had been cancelled.

Three bales of hay were stacked inside the door. A big red hand-lettered sign stuck in one of them said Oregon, Home Sweet Home.

Dinah, wearing her grandmother's long brown skirt, was staring at the sign. She pulled the flaps of her Hot Wheels sunbonnet close over her ears to cut the sound. Then she glanced at the murals of mountains, rivers, and covered wagons that were taped along all the walls. They'd painted them in art class on long rolls of shelf paper. Mostly the mountains looked like rows of tents dipped in marshmallow.

Suddenly it was dark. Kaat had put her hands over Dinah's eyes.

"Let me guess," said Dinah. "It's...Elvis Presley."

"Close," Kaat told her. "He would have loved Oregon, though. The hills are alive with the *pound* of music."

"I just walked in from Missouri and, boy, are my feet tired." Zach joined them. "Where was all this hay yesterday when we needed it? My oxen would have died happy."

Near them, a group of kids were gathered around a bulletin board. The sign on it said WOW! PHOTOS WOW! And underneath were pictures of the pioneer couples taken on that first day, almost two weeks ago.

"Check this out," Kaat told Dinah. "Doesn't look much like Lydia, does it?"

"I hope not." The camera had caught perfectly one of Dinah's top ten dino-faces.

"Or Dr. Jones, either, do you think?" Sarah asked, peering over Kaat's shoulder.

Orin looked like a five-year-old who'd dropped his ice cream in the sand.

"Our picture is gone," Kaat noticed. "Charles must have taken it. I hope so. Listen, Mrs. Jones, I'm going to go catch my train. See you after school."

"Okay, we'll do something."

"Something," Kaat said, "that's not green."

"You think anyone would notice if I just tore our picture into a billion pieces?" a girl asked. "Spike was lazy as a cat. It was not a happy marriage."

Marilou arrived. She was wearing a big straw sunhat, a long full skirt, and a lacy apron that must have belonged to her great grandmother. Like a lot of kids, she'd dressed up for the last day.

"They're really, really awful pictures," she said.

"Not all of them," Dinah told her. "Yours isn't. You're smiling."

"That's because I didn't know what was going to happen. I mean, picking up those buffalo chips and dying and all."

"Except for the dying part, it was kind of fun," Dinah said. "Didn't you think?"

"I guess." Marilou shrugged. "You weren't such a bad leader, mostly."

"Kaat's coming over after school. Maybe if—" Dinah began.

Marilou's eyes skipped right past her. "You're *hee-re!*" She threw her arms around Brandi and Tiffani's shoulders and they hurried off toward the food table.

"Aren't you glad that's over," Brandi asked Marilou. "If anybody calls me Charity one more time, I'll die. I mean it."

"It's not such a bad name," Marilou told her. "Besides, you died anyway."

"Buttermilk corncakes, get 'em while they're hot," Mr. Marconi called from the food line.

"Apple butter for the weary traveler. Warm, spicy apple butter!" Meg stood beside him, spooning it onto yellow paper plates. "And there's genuine homemade pumpkin butter."

Dinah shrugged and peered closer at the pictures.

"Funny, even after two thousand miles, you look exactly the same," said Orin, walking up beside her. He had a way-big cowboy hat on his head and a red and white kerchief tied around his neck. "Except now you're maybe a little..."

"Greener," she said. "And you, of course, are taller." She patted the top of his hat.

"The green's almost gone," he told her.

"Not enough. My brother loves it. But my mother's coming back tomorrow. She'll be mad."

"You think so? I can't think why. Listen, I'm hungry. You hungry?" They headed off to the food table.

"Oh, by the way, one thing I'm very glad about," Dinah said, "and I know you are, too, is that we left Buster in Walla Walla with those nice people."

"You're glad we *what*?" He stopped, but when she didn't, he ran to catch up with her. "Wait a minute. We didn't leave Buster anywhere. He went down the chute with us. What nice people?"

"Oh, didn't I tell you? I thought I mentioned it. At the last minute I saved him."

"You did not. You couldn't have saved him. We didn't even *stop* in Walla Walla."

"Did, too. Buster lives on."

"What about Mildred Erika? You saved your very bright but extremely bratty brother and you let our beautiful Mildred Erika perish in a snowstorm?"

"Mildred Erika was much too little to leave in Walla Walla. Besides, in Walla Walla I didn't know the avalanche would get us."

Mr. Marconi handed her a paper plate of corncakes.

"May I have one more? Thanks," she said. "I'm a growing girl."

"No apple butter for me," Orin told Meg. "Let me try the pumpkin, though."

"How many prairie dogs?" Meg asked.

"Prairie dogs?"

"Link sausages."

"Doubles on apple butter," Dinah told Meg. "A trio of prairie dogs, and hold the pumpkin stuff. I helped make it, so I know what it tastes like." She poured maple syrup over the cornmeal pancakes, sat down at the nearest table, and began to eat.

"May I have your attention," Ms. Stefanik called after a few minutes. She was clapping her hands to the music. "As soon as you've finished breakfast, will Wagon Trains Five and Seven please gather at the south wall. As old-time Oregonians, you're first up to dance. You're going to show those new settlers what a terrific place they've come to."

"She's never seen me dance, or she wouldn't say that," Orin told Dinah.

"We better get this over with," said Dinah, standing up with her empty plate.

"Don't tell the rest of the train you saved Buster," Orin warned her. "They'll say you just made it up."

"That's okay. I did. We made it *all* up. It doesn't matter, anyway. No more wagon leader and good doctor. We're almost back to the real stuff again—Dinahsaurus and the Dork."

She held the yellow plate on top of her sunbonnet and took a giant step. "You want to see Dinah Barnes's new walk? It's guaranteed to make you laugh. And wait till you get a look at this one." She crossed one eye. "I'm putting together my best prehistoric face ever."

17

☞Now Everybody Smile

"Listen up, Wagon Train Seven," Ms. Stefanik began.

"*Ex*-Wagon-Train Seven," Orin called over the sound of the music.

"Quite so. Ex. You're old-time settlers now. Since you were the first ones here, you get to be the first dancers."

"Like that's some kind of reward?" Marilou asked.

"Absolutely," said Ms. Stefanik. "And Ex-Wagon-Train Five will be first to play the jug band instruments."

Brandi, Tiffani, and the rest of the old

Number Five were hovering around Meg, who was explaining how to blow notes out of jugs, strum thimbles on washboards, plunk washtub cellos, and make weird sounds from cross-cut saws. Not likely to make the top forty.

"I'd rather dance," Dinah said.

Ms. Stefanik nodded and clicked a knob on the big black boom box.

The music stopped and so did the talking, all at once, as if the switch had worked on the kids, too.

The microphone hummed.

"My, that silence feels good," said Mr. Marconi. "First of all, I'd like to congratulate you. You did it. You made it all the way to Oregon just like that fine fellow Barney Bilkum said you would. Some of you had big trouble along the way, but, of course, so did some of the pioneers. We're assuming that those of you who threw sixes really made it here earlier and are ready now to lead us all in the big hoedown."

Jessica raised her hand. "Since we got

here first, does that mean we get an A plus? I was just wondering."

"We're not thinking about grades right now, we're thinking about celebrating," Mr. Marconi told her.

"Easy for him to say," Clyde mumbled.

"All of those folk dances you've been practicing in gym class, we're going to do every one right now. We've got 'Bird in the Cage' and 'Dive for the Oyster.' But we're going to start off with the 'Virginia Reel.' "

"Time for the head couple to head out," Ms. Stefanik told ex-Wagon-Train Seven. "Who's it going to be?"

"Head couple?" Dinah asked.

"To lead the 'Virginia Reel.' Who'll you choose?"

"Clyde and Jessica," said Orin. "They're the happiest to get this over with."

"No way," Clyde said. "Unless you really want us to."

"No way," said Jessica. "Unless..."

"You are absolutely right," Marilou said. "You'd be all wrong."

"Not me," Zach said. "I never can

remember my sashay from my do-si-do."

"I'm putting on the music," Ms. Stefanik told them. "You better decide fast."

"I know," said Michael. "Lydia and Dr. Jones. They did the most."

"You're right," Marilou agreed. "They really, really should."

Dinah straightened her shoulders and stepped forward.

"It's decided, then," Ms. Stefanik told them. "Form your two facing lines, Dinah and Orin at the head." She turned the music on again, so loud that first graders on the other side of the school could hum to it.

All the kids in Ex-Wagon-Train Seven headed to the middle of the multipurpose room. All except Orin. He leaned against the wall and crossed his arms.

Dinah ran back to get him. "Come on," she said. "They want us."

"Not me," he told her. He tilted his cowboy hat over his forehead. "I refuse to dance with a stupid-walking weird-faced Dinahsaurus."

Dinah stared. That was mean. Orin had called her a praying mantis that time, a long tall bug, but that was funny mostly. This was *mean*. Still, she grinned at him. Maybe it was a joke.

He did not grin back.

"But I want to," she said. "And they want us to. This is the last of the good part."

"Nope," he said, sounding like a cowboy in an old Western. "Unless. The only way I will is if you promise to stop the dumb walks and the stupid faces."

"I won't do them *now*," she said. "Not now."

"Not ever. Promise."

"What's going *on*?" Clyde called. The others were standing in the middle of the room in two straight lines. "If you don't lead, Jessica and I will."

"Please," Dinah said.

"Will you quit the dinosaur stuff?" he asked.

"I can't. That's who I *am*," she said.

The music stopped.

"Lead couple take your places," Mr. Marconi called. "What's your problem?"

"I'll try," Dinah told Orin.

"Not good enough."

"Okay, okay, I promise."

"Cross your heart?"

"Or-*in!*" Dinah shouted, and the music began again.

The jug band was thwonking out beeps and peeps and thunks and ka-chunks.

"Di-*nah!*" Kaat called. She and Charles were clapping.

"Okay, I cross," said Dinah, and she did. She ran to the head of the line. Orin followed.

"And here we go!" The music stopped and began again from the beginning. Mr. Marconi made the calls.

Dinah and Orin went forward.

Dinah and Orin came back. Her bonnet flew loose and her green hair bounced like little springs. Orin's big hat stayed put, but Dinah was still taller.

"Right arm swing," Mr. Marconi called. And they swung. Left arm swing, right arm swing, do-si-do. They reeled.

The next time Orin and Dinah hooked arms she said, "It's no fair, though."

"What's no fair?"

But she swung on to Clyde before she could answer. Clyde seemed to be liking this part. He whooped as he danced.

Then it was time to make the arch. Dinah and Orin held up their hands for the others to duck under.

"No fair," she said to Orin, "is that I have to stop making my great faces and walking my amazing walks, and you're still a dork." If that was mean, it was okay with Dinah.

"You know you shouldn't make them laugh at you," he told her. "Not like that."

"Sure," she said. "Thanks a lot." But she didn't mean it.

They stepped back into their separate lines and watched Marilou and Michael go forward and back as the new head couple. The jug band was losing steam, but the dancers weren't. And the whole fifth grade was watching and clapping.

Except for Kaat and Charles in the front

row. Kaat was holding out a big loop of red string, trying to teach Charles how to make a cat's cradle.

When the dance was over and the reel spun out, Mr. Marconi said, "Hurrah! That was swell. Let's give our old-time settlers here a great big hand."

And as they did, Orin stepped forward to Dinah. He pulled off his hat, and he bowed.

Once again, for a nanosecond, the multipurpose room was dead quiet because of Orin.

"I don't believe it," said Dinah. "I don't believe it."

But it was true. Believe it or not.

Orin's hair was purple. Under the cowboy hat all that morning, Orin's hair had been vivid purple. Grape. He smiled.

Kids laughed. But they didn't go crazy. It wasn't like before, when he'd swallowed Dinah's name to keep from marrying her. He just had purple hair, that's all.

Mr. Marconi wasn't going to yell at him. He wasn't about to let this spoil his party.

"Those folks out west," he said. "They were rugged individualists. Hard to tell what they'd do next. But one thing they liked to do was dance. So, everybody out on the floor."

He nodded to Ms. Stefanik and she started up the music. "We're going to 'Dive for the Oyster' now," he said. "You remember that one. All join hands."

"I thought for sure you'd notice that I smell like a snow cone," said the purple-haired boy to the green-haired girl. "Do I still look like a nerd?"

Dinah smiled. "A little. Maybe not. Did your mother let you do that?"

"She doesn't know. I rubbed the stuff on just before I left. My hair's still wet. I think it froze on the way to school."

"You'll catch a cold."

"I don't know. I made it all the way to Oregon without one."

"We didn't really make it."

"Sort of. Not like the rest of them, but we're here."

"Dive for the oyster, dive," Mr. Marconi

called out. "Dig for the clam, now dig. Dive for your home and a happy land."

"And smile," Meg called. She was aiming a video camera at the dancers. "You're starting a brand new life. Smile."

They all smiled. Some of them made crazy faces at the camera. But not all. Not the green-haired girl dancing with the grape-haired boy.

About the Author

"'I know why you write about us,' a sixth-grade boy once told me. 'It's because we're middle-aged and things are happening to us.' And it's true. My characters are all in the process of growing up, of being astonished by the strange way their world works.

"You can see yourself and your weaknesses in someone else as easily when you are laughing at his muddle as when you are weeping at his despair. That's what I try to do—make my readers laugh and understand at the same time.

"Before writing I always do research. I've talked to boys about collecting beer cans, to refugees about what it was like coming to America, to teachers of children with learning disabilities. I once went with a class to outdoor education camp. I've asked kids what it was like to be in programs for the gifted and talented. It is this close observation that I hope makes my books seem real."

Born in Beardstown, Illinois, Jamie Gilson spent her early years in several small midwestern towns where her father worked as a flour miller. After graduating from Northwestern University, she married Jerome Gilson, then a law student and now a trademark lawyer. In addition to writing, Mrs. Gilson has worked as a junior high school speech and English teacher, a staff writer and producer for the Division of Radio and Television of the Chicago Public Schools, and served as continuity director for radio station WFMT. The Gilsons have three grown children, Tom, Matthew, and Anne, and live in a suburb of Chicago.